STAR QUILT
(THE SEVENTH JUMP)

A fictional story of
Little Norway, Minnesota

Lynn Strongin

Plain View Press
P. O. 42255
Austin, TX 78704

plainviewpress.net
sb@plainviewpress.net
512-441-2452

ISBN: 978-0-9819731-8-0
Library of Congress Number: 2009925825

Cover photo by Deborah Munro.
Cover design by Susan Bright.

Acknowledgments

Many thanks to my copy editor, Kathryn Kuchenbrod, and to Megan Bright for proof reading.

For my photographer and life companion, D,

and for my younger sister, Debbie

Contents

Part One

Chapter One — Albino Fox   11
Chapter Two — The Moment to Be Most Alive   17
Chapter Three — What Genius Has Old Age?   25
Chapter Four — Gun-shy: Frozen Letter Carrier   31
Chapter Five — Flames and Red Stockings   45
Chapter Six — Celibacy and Cold Water   55
Chapter Seven — Not to Die Must Have Been the Goal   61
Chapter Eight — Lars   69
Chapter Nine — The Lack of Crystalline   73
Chapter Ten — When There's an Explosion, All the Birds Fly   81
Chapter Eleven — Red Feather Duster   85
Chapter Twelve — Runners and Nuns   89
Chapter Thirteen — A Whole New Set of Listeners   93

Part Two

Chapter Fourteen — In the Cabin (Under Silver and Low Sky)   97
Chapter Fifteen — Our Towhee   105
Chapter Sixteen — An Iridescent Quality   119
Chapter Seventeen — It's Venison, My Love   123
Chapter Eighteen — Gone Canoeing   125
Chapter Nineteen — Sleep Like a Child Under Your Needs   127

Part Three

Chapter Twenty — The Letters   135
Chapter Twenty-one — Rachel Reads   137
Chapter Twenty-two — Early Stills   141
Chapter Twenty-three — The Stone Eyeball   143
Conclusion — The Final Stills   147

About the Author   155

In old age, we must have reached the confidence to speak our hearts.

—Jane Rule

As cotton fabric became more available commercially in the first half of the nineteenth century, women were freed to experiment with a wonderful variety of colors and prints in their quilt-making. A good example of the creativity this made possible can be found in a distinctive star quilt made with one large star covering most of the quilt top.

Nobody knows that she lies there but her hawk and her hound and her lady fair.

—Old English Ballad

PART ONE

Chapter One
Albino Fox

The stars that covered Chel were just cloth, but they gave light. The room was wood; it sheltered her. Now that the love of her life had left a year ago Christmas, she wore the old quilt like a cape.

In the seventh jump, when the cord rope whacked on the dirt of the grammar school playground, the faces of the children tightened, blanched as if bleached with white flour or dusted with death itself. The superstition was that if you missed this one, bad luck would be yours. In the seventh jump of life, the faces Chel saw about her were preparing for eternity.

She didn't know the woman in the mirror. She felt she had had a spear driven through a hole in her chest. Formerly the postmaster in the town of a little more than ten thousand souls, Little Norway in northern Minnesota on the teal Boundary Waters that border Canada, Rachel was about to turn seventy. She inhabited their home of many years; it had become a forest, the dark woods, the home they'd named "Widdershins." Time running backward, Maggie and Rachel had chosen the name Widdershins for the weather-beaten homestead that appeared an ancient tall master shipwreck. Chel was also keeping vigil, an eye open for Maggie's possible return.

Rachel wore Maggie's star quilt like a cape. There were small windows in its stained-glass colors now; the bold quilted squares of purple and cobalt had become thread-thin. It belonged to Europe now with the resonance of Spain and Italy, its old bellowers, brick belfries, crumbling sepia stars. The star quilt was covered with eight-pointed stars cut up from old nightgowns that had a milky, silvery satin on the reverse side that suggested snow and was now sister to greatcoats, to ice and wind, cousin to steeplejacks. The old comforter brought Rachel no comfort. It was the spirit that goes, the body keeps on breathing. A river ran through town. The river's private name to Rachel was Peace. Chel lost sight of it in her sixty-ninth year and would gain sight again in her seventieth.

*

She'd gone through wearing all of Maggie's sweaters: the barn-red cardigan, the dark green pullover with patched elbows, the gray cardigan were all too tight to button; the cuffs rode up three inches above her wrist. She, who had become a hermit and an Ishmael, sought a miracle. She slept in the faded raspberry counterpane as though it were a nest and trawled it about the house as though it were a cloak of sun-bleached stars. Bleached, it still shed light as though a map of the stars, a planetarium sky had spilled over her in rich northern light. Crumpled star constellations folded and unfolded as she breathed. A block of writing paper stood at her elbow. She wanted to write, but it was too cold to write. Years ago, she had held up the brandy; firelight shone through its stained glass.

"Maggie, do I drink too much?"

"You are in pain."

Snow clouds rolled over, big-shouldered buffalo. Scorned as timber, beloved of sky, Rachel was six feet tall, weather-beaten. Little Norway was blessed with great choirs and clear northern water. "You are Rembrandt in his self portrait," Maggie said. "You are his son Titus in your crushed black beret." Maggie in her sixties with blonde bangs and Rachel at near seventy with a brooding expression did resemble Rembrandt and Titus, the way Jewish faces haunted Rembrandt in his quarter of Holland. No longer were the strange, haunting bells from the old Lutheran church to be heard. The bell ringer had quit last December. The church had parishioners going back three generations, parishioners who had boyhood and girlhood imaginations fueled by Hans Christian Andersen's tales. Little Norway belonged to both Andersen and Isak Dinesen's Gothic fairy-tale imagination.

Snow brushed like a broom against the windowpane of Widdershins, a snow scythe swung with an ominous sound, a mythical swan in the night. In the corner near the piano were her work gloves, ash-blue, caked with mud from the garden. Burleson, the old sheepdog, stirred in the corner, too tired to turn over in dreaming. Both dog and woman were maladjusted after Maggie's abandonment. Rachel ran her hand through her silver shag, the silver that led Maggie to nickname her "Albion Fox," after her favorite country. Britain was a land Rachel, too, loved: that stubborn rock that was a geographic equivalent to her own stubbornness. When the lights had blown out, she drove to town for a ton of candles. The entire town was in the general store buying flashlights, batteries, oil lamp mantles, and fuel.

Chel gazed out upon the frozen potting shed, recalling the outhouse of her girlhood where there was scant privacy. Like the woodshed, it was surrounded with the smoky fear of the unknown. In the shed this frozen night the tools, too, were frozen in their irons: precise, each shaped to a purpose like clockwork parts. The rust-colored birdhouse was bearded with icicles. It was precisely one year ago this night Maggie had packed tripods, camera bodies and lenses, rising glass-like upon the even glassier night, Maggie had packed her gear, windbreakers, smocks and all. She stood there like a sixty-eight-year-old child in her earth boots and red woolen socks when she took leave of Widdershins. In addition to keeping her vigil, Rachel reasoned, I have my blue-heron nun, Josephine, Jo, Josepha, whose half-smile goes with her being tall and thus able to fold her body into chairs. And for hardship, humility, the rough-hewn blessing. These were late day's white-hot coals: the last embers often give the most intense heat. She shoved a log in the fire and lay back, her face reflecting a life deeply lived, maps of mourning and of ecstasy in it, a geography. She made herself smile recalling Maggie, icicles stuck to her tongue from licking an iron post. She had memories of the glories of the dime store, Hendrickson's down the street, where in heavy blizzards the two women trekked for last-minute Christmas gifts.

They were so far north that the sky was as tarnished as the family silver. What one person resented you for, chances were others liked about you. Chel's silence was punctuated by the Norwegian grandfather clock of dark wood with glass face and Roman numerals in the hallway. Its tick tock grew louder when the silent hours came. Jars of winter crab apple and quince jelly were so bright that they caught the light like a church window. There was a winter pomegranate Maggie found and had meant to split in half and photograph. She feared the seventh hour each morning and each evening. It made her think of that treacherous seventh jump of the skipping rope on girlhood's playground, an omen now as she entered her seventieth year in life. She experienced a sense of fright every year at this time she had never become familiar with. It came with the winter solstice. She drew the comforter closer about her; it had marks from children's jam-stained hands on it and rips where sheepdog Burleson had slept on it. In fact, the quilt was engraved with history and geography like a globe. Rachel had a private gospel: letters were her Holy Grail. She sat by the window, unable to see farther than the blue icy drive. She brought out of the closet and stood against various walls the bold canvases she liked that Maggie did not. The quilt was mainly dusty with Holland blue stars, raspberry flowers made of old nightgowns. In the last years of the twentieth century, she might have been a wayfarer in the Middle Ages.

Her garden gloves become her signature just as Maggie's hallmark had been Gauloises or the Sobranies Black Russian cigarettes they had smoked together for decades. She wouldn't know until after New Year the results of the ultrasound, which showed a spot on one lung. Maggie had nicknamed Chel Albion Fox, but she felt like the name's inversion, the Albino Fox, when she turned the comforter the other way around. The nether side was stitched antique satin; once white, it now had the luster of a silver patina. She had a vision of Dolly, her twin, who long ago drowned in childhood on a summer afternoon. Flooded in childhood, the girl surfaced tonight. Revenant, Dolly would remain forever platinum, a ribbon in her hair turned to floating pearl. Sheltering yet shuddering under the quilt, Rachel recalled with the vividness as if a match had lit the scene—those trunks her father and mother had with the pullout drawers: the twins adored those trunks. They would build constructs out of childhood's imagination. Her six-foot frame shifted around, a bulk like a mountain or a cloud as if of its own accord. Other than that, there was little movement.

*

A swatch of cobalt satin, a silvery oyster triangle and a triangle of emerald velvet: these had once been the colors of the counterpane. The silence was as heavy as lead, as pewter covered the rooms. She would have preferred sound to this silence, perhaps the needle biting into the old vinyl of Pachebel's canon. She would have preferred Dolly alive rather than revenant, as the dead are called when they pay their visits. She spoke to herself in the voice that came up from the grave.

They had dwelt in north light. No magnifying glass would start a fire in this sun. There was the old pew Maggie had rescued from the church rummage sale in order to paint in the colors and style of Sweden: glossy crimson with vellum background, bringing out convoluted sepia roses scrolled along the top and on either side. The church bench looked like wings, dramatic, as though the wood was crying Alarm! Alarm! Maggie had been a visionary of the sky carving paths in the cream of fresh snow. Transfixing, terrific, she trespassed all rules in order to shoot a photograph. Give her two planks and she had a passion. Give her an egg cup and she had a bookmark photograph.

Nobody knows that she lies there but her hawk and her hound and her lady fair.

*

Whence sight for this blind? Burleson, the ancient sheepdog stirred in the corner of their room piled with books. There was the bag on which Mag had embroidered "One cannot have too many books," with a drawing of a woman and books piled every which way.

It was so cold that the air rang like a chime—the illimitable twenty-third of December.

She repeated images to herself like a lesson she had learned in Sunday school. She said it with an outside, narrating voice. Half a century ago in the coziest nightgowns in the Midwest, trailers, very long and very old flannel nightgowns worn by little girls in Minnesota who had turned nine and ten. I have my blue heron nun, Josephine; she smiled a half-smile. Jo was tall enough to fold into chairs gracefully. And for hardship, humility, the rough-hewn blessing. These nights were white-hot coals: embers give the most intense heat. She shoved a log and lay back, her seventy-year-old face reflecting a life deeply lived, maps of mourning and of ecstasy in it, a geography.

In the days before Christmas was the time when, as postmaster, Chel felt the greatest loss. Little Norway's Lutheran Church had lost their bell ringer of thirty years at precisely this time last year. Rachel had learned to find solitude luminous when Maggie left after thirty years. Maggie, with her Swedish bowl haircut and her smile, was as honest as the day is long.

Her pulse quickened. The snow was thick as white woodchips, and she felt the creative anxiety one feels as the winter solstice nears, especially when there's a full moon. Little Norway had a population of fewer than ten thousand. Alone all day with only the buzz of the generator, the blue glass outside with icicles on it, Rachel mused. She was forever reading *London War Notes*, by Mollie Panter-Downes, a collection of letters written for *The New Yorker* during World War II. It was a book she and Margaret read aloud to one another. Last year she had moved for one month to a bed-sitter in the liver-colored October Mansion in the original town square of Little Norway, but it had not worked out, so she moved back to Widdershins. In it she thought she could travel the full three hundred sixty degrees of her longing, but she was stuck at about ten degrees. Like a frozen sundial, she did not move. She knocked back a shot of brandy, sweeping her silver bangs from her eyes. The bright colors of the quilt, originally Amish hues, had faded to the dusty rose, teal, and celadon of comforters she had seen in Europe. Rachel had her autocracy, her austereness. With a tendency to overwhelm—her tall frame, which equipped her well for the post office, could shade all at a gathering—she figured she'd been born to lead whether or not she had followers. Her strong alto, her stride, and her instincts of a guiding mother like Karyn, her own mother, contributed to the powerful presence. She wore gray to play down her own nature.

Maggie's goal was to capture American small towns and frame them in a silvery photograph. The shape of American towns was in her bones. Her move out from Widdershins, like her work, had been bold but not mutinous. Tonight tree skeletons rattled in the Arctic blue of Minnesota not far from the Boundary Waters, which divided Northern Minnesota from Canada. Earlier this evening, children's voices had risen. Kids had beat sticks on parchment and piped flutes, which gave their performance a medieval spin. Little Norway looked like a medieval town etched in cold crystal. It could have been, in fact, an etching of an Albrecht Dürer town. The city was all bones, profiles of churches, and town hall, houses and school: the skyline was tower-choked. Public and private buildings shone.

A dog barked. Then all was still.

The couriers had delivered their parcels. The streets were silent. Ribbons of silver-blue snow and ice.

"Scorned as timber, beloved of sky," Rachel was a survivor: tall, weather-beaten. Caring for the community kept her from giving into the impulse to draw an igloo around herself. "You look like Rembrandt van Rijn in his last self-portraits," Maggie would claim, pointing the figure at her awesome love. "And you like his young son Titus in that black velvet beret of yours," Rachel would respond. A sharpness had come into her tone after that first spot which was found to be benign was found. It would have been nice to have family in the wings: instead she had her listeners, Little Norway's community of women.

Maggie and Rachel had faces that haunted the community. No longer did the church bells haunt the community. The old Lutheran church bells were no longer to be heard. The church had parishioners dating back three generations, parishioners whose imaginations were vivid with folklore and fairy tale. The town had a shipwreck horizon; Little Norway belonged to both Andersen and Isak Dinesen. Rachel closed the covers of both books now, as it were. Her hand had canceled generations of letters; her index finger was permanently scarred despite the thimble she used. Always known as tallest, calmest of them all, Rachel had exemplified endurance.

Ach well, in my criticism, Rachel thought, rising, I could have been more gentle, and, Maggie, you could have been less sharp with your tongue even though, with your artist's eye, you saw more things than most of us. Protective women like I was were your favorites. It could all be taken in a twinkling. Rachel remembered that she was waiting over Christmas for the results of her ultrasound. At the end, Rachel summed up, I imagine it seems as though I was she who must be obeyed, trying to control Maggie for as long we had kept each other's ragged company. It was my latent insecurity, which I should have solved on my own. We both exploded. All I wanted was a line drawing of a church vault.

Chapter Two

The Moment to Be Most Alive

"Look!" Maggie points, "A blur of silk is on the sky. A dolphin."
Click.

Days later, a white pitcher stands in the bathroom against a silver
winter sky almost the color of chalk. A hand-tinted sky. The terrible
thing about you, Maggie, was the little boy in you. The toughie at five-
foot-three, she put her hands on her hips, in bib overalls, film cans
spilling out of her pockets, and took my heart and spun it. The terrible
thing about you is it wasn't a matter of let the dog out, bring the wash
in, but across-the-board emotional demands: the hose you wore, the
velveteen stockings, the cross-gartered tights of the fool were merely
symbolic of the larger design underneath.

We gandered at everything: the hurricane missing its mark, the coins
in the bright red letterbox bank. The potting shed or the outhouse—what
was more private in our girlhood? The fear surrounding Christmas.

We bantered until each one was she who must be obeyed, and
there was anarchy. The only thing to obey is the law of the light. Each
became caricatures of who we are. She outshone the clown. I outdarked
midnight. "The story city," I think, is what she was magnetized by in the
vivid paintings of the fairy-tale artist and what I ought to have seen. The
children at potato play, throwing a hot spud back and forth, charmed
and enchanted both Maggie and me. Being with her in a snowstorm was
the most romantic thing I could imagine.

Jo was as lean as a greyhound. Her decisive living gave her the lean
physique of a thin boxer. She had a pre-Raphaelite profile. Her light
brown curls were in the style that was once called crimped, and she had
an aquiline nose. Jo freed herself of the convent's enclosure and took up
life with Harriet, a lawyer and champion of women's rights. Jo, a former
Franciscan, had the map of Ireland written on her face and was keenly
conscious that the fox had his den, the bird his nest, but the son of man
(daughter of woman) had not where to lay his head.

Rachel returned most often to Jo's words, to Maggie's photographs as
she neared the decade, which brought confidence and freedom to voice
her feelings.

"Sky looks hand-tinted," Margaret would say. It was gathering wool
flakes behind the pitcher-porcelain horizon, like candles that Maggie had
set on the sill. Rachel yearns to see a smudge of cobalt or lilac, even red
in the photographs. The yearning gets the better of her at times. "Why

not give color a go?" Maggie shook her head. She had selected north light, which cast no shadows.

The handtinted photograph of the pitcher darkened. A wood-burning fire was roaring in their room at the time.

She went out and did a shoot of her favorite hill with graves on one side gathering ice. On the opposite side stood Little Norway Fish Market. For years Maggie and Rachel had had taped on their refrigerator: SEVEN DAYS WITHOUT FISH MAKES ONE WEAK.

With another swish of the shutter, Maggie took the rare self-portrait. She did look a bit like Rembrandt's Titus; her face at sixty was weathered, handsome in the warped bathroom mirror, which made one eye a bit higher than the other. Maggie had eyes the color of rain.

*

Sipping brandy together, Jo and Rachel smiled, "It goes down easily with you, Chel." Jo is the only person who calls Rachel that. They came of age when stockings and chocolate were rationed, when Roosevelt's Fireside Chats transfixed the nation in front of huge old Stromberg-Carlsons. The bulldog's boom from Britain rumbled across the ocean on watery sound waves.

After Mag's departure, Rachel found the clarity to speak without halting came hard. Maggie had stuttered as a hoydenish girl. She overcame it, but the stutter came back the winter before her leaving. Her nails were bloody, bitten down. As she spoke with Jo, Rachel pictured the stone angels floating before her eyes as though they were airbrushed, not made of stone. Graveyard angels filled the home along with tripods and lenses. Maggie had a library of books by women photographers: Dorothea Lange, Imogen Cunningham, Annie Leibowitz. There were contact sheets by the score and acid baths. Rachel thrilled to the creativity hatching under her wing. At the same time, it grated against her sense of economy. She was hard-wired to fear loss. Hers had been the last age to cling to the belief that a war could be won. Hers was not a totally rational grief. She rose to grab the kettle when she heard someone shriek, "Shut up, Eliot!" as in T.S. Eliot. The world would end with a whimper not a bang. Their john had been a darkroom—ironing board stashed in the tub, enlarger on the side of the sink.

"You don't know," Rachel said to Jo, "when you fall permanently in love."

"No. Often love changes."

"All I have left is to contemplate," Rachel thought, recalling something Ezra Pound once said. She studied the floor planks, the wood

shining through like butter, like little lamps. She held a winter apple in
her hands, then set it down on the sill where the sun lit it up to crimson
fire.

Permanently in love. The love merely changes. It's strange to have no
more unsafe silence to weave around in the home. The interiors of their
rooms died slowly in her eye. When Maggie had left, she wore her gray-
blonde hair in a shingle. It resembled sun-bleached wood. She still wore
railroad pants, parachute pants, occasionally smocks with pockets to stash
cans of film. Rachel hoped that she would not be called out tonight in
this freeze. She was the town exterminator. She had no sidekick. CERTIFIED
PESTICIDE DISPENSER read the button she was obliged to wear. She kept her
real estate license current as well. These were jobs for dabbling in after
retirement. She sold only the occasional piece of property now, since the
recession began. She missed the smell of Maggie's Gauloises, smoked one
after another. She missed the rough tobacco, the bicycle with its reflecting
surfaces in the hall propped against the leaning bookcase. She has left a
night light burning in the socket where she plugged in the toaster. With
its hood, the light reminded one of a falcon. She knew the grid of town
streets by heart; her feet had memorized them. She saw them now, closing
her eyes to the hot tea. Too much brandy. The grid sweeping to north,
east, south and west, like their lives. She still called a suitcase a valise, a
phone a telephone. She came close to becoming a telephone operator
when she was a child. In her sixteenth year she switched her dream job
to the post office. Those small dovecotes haunted her dreams. That brass
set of vertical bars, a grille, silken to the touch haunted her too. The town
map, the wrong side of the tracks and the wrong side of the heart.

Rachel recited passages from the *London War Journal* as though it was
a Bible. She recalled the day when the newspaper ran a Bible names
game contest and how infuriated her mother had been that she had not
won. Although London may not be precisely comfortable, it is at the
moment one of the most exhilarating cities in the world. Rachel's hands
were folded on her breast. Quoting from the book, she felt like a very old
child reciting in a strange bygone school. She was being schooled for the
seventh jump, the great war of old age, the need for affection wrestling the
instinct for survival.

What did afflict Maggie and me? Was it simply cabin fever? But why so
late in the day? It was as though something essential dissolved: that fine
line that one can never see or touch but is palpable in the air. I think of
that Russian headline from ten years back: BED LINEN IS NOT BEING CHANGED
AND THE PEOPLE ARE MISERABLE. In our case, we exemplified the saying,
"Threatened people show their worst side." If we ever come together
again, which I hope we will, I shall be gentler.

She opened the black journal for her journey, lighting a Diamond match to read the conclusion of the passage in *London War Journal* that she had underscored. She'd marked the page with a burnt match:

The everyday things of life ... thrown out of gear by events are in order again. Mr. Malcolm McDonald said that if he could choose the moment in which he most wanted to be alive, he would choose a few days or a few weeks hence ... whenever the enemy would strike with ... maximum force against this island.

Twice alive. Fighting in this cold to keep alive? The everyday things of life had gone askew. She crawled out of bed, dragging the star quilt with her everywhere. She turned up the heat register first thing on getting up. They had their rituals, as did a community of nuns. But who was mother superior? Had the power balance in their love simply changed? If so, why this magnum thrust, this great turnabout of emotion? Patience. *Patience and Sarah*, I twig. I must pull that glowing novel from the shelf again. It should be flying off the shelf at this point. To the rescue, like Hook & Ladder Company No. 9.

With the heat register up, the old pipes bubble like an undersea diver. I feel I am a diver undersea. I keep my eyeballs fastened to the door. Moments later, pipes bang like small drummer boys hidden in the old radiator pipes. She recalled setting out her clothing on the pipes as a child. Widdershins. Things now were Widdershins. The enemy had struck. But name the enemy. Although Maggie's leaving has been a stunner, there had been a series of warnings. I need to take a train journey alone across the country. "How can you afford to?" Mag had shrugged in that way that maddened Rachel, like a cross between a child and a temperamental diva. But she, too, needed time alone, the retired postmaster. They both did: Rachel to see the world within her histories, the thousands of postage stamps, Maggie to see the winter world through glass. Winter was Maggie's season. Dream. Make necessary connections. She could comprehend being excluded. The community had loved her and Maggie equally, but now all but Jo had somewhat shut her out. It was a thing hard to point to but something she could tell, a thing she could nearly palpate.

We had another controversial, long-standing dream: Maggie wanted to add a greenhouse to our home. We couldn't afford both the rail trip and the greenhouse. I used my persuasive powers two years ago. I brought them fully to bear. I had seen through the project of erecting Maggie's greenhouse wing, however. There it stands, the glass pitted by ice, by wind. Inside stand the blasted seedlings.

Earlier than the rail trip, Margaret knew I had had a plea: to spend
a full calendar year in England. That's my baby, my white-haired boy or
girl.

"Well, look, I brought us apricot boats," Mag boasted, holding the
heavy English pastries. "Two boats each." Rachel shook her head. Maggie
had only a half-sabbatical from teaching high school art. Funds ran thin.
Since it was impossible for Rach to obtain working papers in England,
that dream had been, as Margaret saw it, brutally whooshed down the
drain. To Maggie this scotched trip to England felt like the final blow.
Actually it was the initial one. Mag had asked to sleep in separate rooms.

That was late September last year, when Margaret struck out for the
wilds of Northern Minnesota to teach a darkroom techniques course.
The instructor had died suddenly. She found the right moment for the
right action.

So we weren't just having a bad patch, Chel went on, extracting the
words with much pain still in her dusky voice, veiled by brandy.

Jo understood. "When I'm angry I go out and lash water. I swim. I
even dislocated a shoulder once doing it."

Jo was the most outspoken of the community of women artists
and artisans in Little Norway. Rachel was the most imposing with her
Churchillian stoop. Quilt makers, potters, weavers all were shaded by
Rachel.

"What's it like up there?" folk would ask.

She would frown. "Tallest is all I've ever known."

She'd sat by the electric fire chatting with Jo. She hated electric logs.
The retired antique collector, whose specialty was rose globes, loved
antique electric logs, but then she was a collector.

Rachel laughed, "If I hadn't become town postmaster, I'd have
been an operator, but I'm not the listening-in kind." She'd licked her
index finger and held it up. The crucifix around her neck had been the
badge of Jo's profession. Rachel recalled handling envelopes with the
cancellation BUY WAR BONDS. With a wide back and powerful hiking
stride, why not carry sacks of mail? She'd loved hiking with her brothers.
She loved receiving letters but was poor at writing them. She reminisced
with Josephine about how the low red-brick grammar school had
changed. She and Maggie hadn't recognized each other until the second
meeting at St. Olaf's College. At grammar school, in the dirt playground
where they'd skipped rope, they did not exchange names, and even those
had been forgotten like an old rubbed-raw coin. On the playground,
superstition ran rife. As children, we believed that if you missed the
seventh jump, something horrendous would happen to you. Maybe the

Death Horse of Norse mythology would come galloping to carry a child away as he had Dorothea, Dolly, Rachel's mirror twin.

Our girlhood was steeped in the mystique of the Death Horse. His truths, triumphant processions, were iridescent, iconic in our dreams. Darlingest, Merry Christmas.

Rachel felt a powerful revival of her drowned twin. Like Ophelia, Dolly drowned. Some people attribute this closeness to the life shared in the womb. Turning around and around in amniotic fluid, twins coexist for months before birth, hands intertwined.

After Jo went back home to Harriet, Rachel felt solitude more sharply than usual. She leafed through personal ads in desultory fashion.

"Small woman seeks woman companion for walks, social drinking." She flung the paper down. She grieved Dolly. She grieved Maggie. She grieved all of them.

Maggie had commanded that she inscribe the following on her tomb: PHOTOGRAPHER & FOLK ARTIST. "It's simple. It suits you," Rach said with pain. She looked back to this and ahead to "Small woman seeks woman companion." Rachel also thought the directive a bit stern.

"Let's start a bookstore," Jo had said (to distract ourselves from grief, the unstated loss). Her statements were always understated as though they were equations, with one half given.

Jo had continued, "I know the perfect loft. We'll call it Histories & Mysteries."

"I know the loft too," Rachel had shaken her head, "but it's too damned expensive. Books are one more luxury I must cut out."

"You'll feet better," Jo tried, "when you come out of hiding."

Rachel was startled as though struck by lightning. "Me? In hiding?"

Tonight, the solstice, running her fingers through Burleson's fur, she said elegiacally, "Soon my old bitch will be dead."

Damned if she would, damned if she wouldn't. A minister's daughter, she willed herself to put her life back within a frame. But she regarded faith with caution. She regarded faith with hesitation, not passion. Her chore was to cook the two fat geese this year for the community of women. She had to get on to the stuffing: bread, nuts, prunes.

Sometimes, around twilight, a spirit hovered near her when she was alone. It was Petré (the Swedish form of Peter) for whom they had turned their hearts inside out. More fools they since in those days no single woman, or pair of them, could adopt. He was blind and had been hospitalized all his life. Mildly spastic, too, Petré had been drowned in freckles at birth.

Petré seemed carved out of the hollowness of grief. Because he was blind, brightly colored maps on clay-based paper pulled down on elastic were denied to him. Math classes were taken from him. The vials of medicines on teal trays that were given to him would never heal him. He would never discover who his mother and father were. They had fallen through the crack in the world from which the light shone. He never had a comfortable childhood, was never guarded by a loving parent. Chel and Maggie adopted him, emotionally and spiritually, although all they could do was visit him in Little Norway's children's hospital, where he had a bed on a ward with ten other kids. He was born with perfect pitch, and when Maggie played the ancient ward piano, he sang along. He sang "Amazing Grace" in a high piping soprano and stopped hearts when Maggie played it on the ancient ward piano. He imitated the orderlies, "Stinks in here," he said, making them all laugh.

In those days, Harriet, that tough unbeliever, was not yet among them with her sharp mind, her keen tongue and raw, clean-cut profile. Daumier's lawyers, *Les Avocats*, were caricatures with elongated figures in sarcastic postures that bore out Harriet to the tee. She had, with wisdom, selected them to line her study. Harriet had the profile of the huntress Diana, with a foxy glance and a Garbo-like manner of moving. She was a clotheshorse. Harriet and Jo had lived together since the day Jo left the convent.

"I'm taking to drink," Rach had said two years ago, when more than winter closed them in. Maggie, however, knew Chel's austerities. "When things get better," Chel had said to Jo, "then we can complain." She used to say this to Maggie. She would sit on the windowsill in those days wearing postal gray, waiting to do night duty. Night sorting was when she felt a peculiar kinship to the men flying above the Atlantic, whose dark waters swirled and churned at night. In the South Pacific, Navy ships fought Japanese destroyers. In the North Atlantic destroyers waited for German submarines to show. Sleepless while others slept. Bombers performed suicide dives. Dolly, she and Amelia Earhart were kin, although it was Maggie who had wanted to take up aviation. The Marines had rigged a poster of woman pilot climbing into a plane, camera in hand.

Of course, Harriet was the great combatant. She conveyed the ardent desire for controversial verbal exchange by becoming a woman lawyer. She relished a good argument. Some of the community voiced the criticism that Harriet conveyed the manners of a temptress. It came from insecurity in childhood, if indeed it was a veiled seduction. There was no more use snapping at her than at a red herring. Her argumentativeness did, however, set some folk on edge. Harriet had a voice that came up from the grave. From the depths of that thin chest, a low voice boomed, struck monotone at times, which must have lulled some in the

courtroom to sleep or near sleep. Jo put one in mind of an actress in
a tragic Russian film. With her pale coloring and fur collar, one could
imagine her sipping the odd vodka at a tearoom called Little Russia.

Jo had a rather high musical soprano and was fond of singing old
English and Irish folk songs, such as "John Barleycorn." Jo had hair like
the silvery cap of the nuthatch. Harriet had turned salt-and-pepper early
with a striking touch of charcoal. Jo's chestnut bob was tipped silver
by her thirties. Her limbs had a nearly translucent quality after a bout
with illness. Her legs and arms appeared marbled after the cloistered
years. Her spine was erect, rigid out of conviction and out of despair
reminiscent of a Giacometti sculpture. Harriet had always been angular,
hypnotic. Was she neurotic as well? In court, her brilliance shone,
giving her a veneer. Passion deepened her already eloquent speech with
awareness how good and evil moved in the courts of the world. She,
above all others, knew that justice was not tempered with mercy. We
are dealt a mixed hand. There is little sense to it. We often play with a
stacked deck.

Icicles hung by the wall. "Who am I?" asked Rachel. As far back as I
can remember, I have had a steady hand. I have been tall. Haven't our
lives been ruled by a heroism of the hand? "Townscape" hung on our
wall, Maggie's and mine, from our twenties on. It is the wool tapestry we
bought when we were flat broke. Out of pocket, we needed "Townscape"
for our home, the American heartland catching and reflecting our
tempers, our tongues. Here is a row of flat brick factories standing like
Manchester Village. In middle distance braided railroad tracks look
like black wool lacing. In the far background, but in front of a red-brick
factory with narrow dark windows, runs a murky stream whose water
powers the mill. What happened to that factory? It has always puzzled
me. Maybe in it linen was woven. Perhaps bricks were made in it. A
foundry. A plate factory. There's a Scandinavian blue-wool sky. Jo's words
blow back to me in the icy wind tonight. "Chel, I have never known two
people more involved than we are with things that are not superficial."

All beautiful, supple animals are now folded away into darkness.
Rachel rinses the dinner dishes with clear, hot water, watching the
grease float off in an envelope. Suddenly, those extraordinary animals
begin rippling, flaming again. If you were a horse and my back right—she
flashed a threatening glance—I'd ride you away. The quilt that she
shook out with its eight-pointed stars began shining: oranges, squares
of midnight black and jade green glistened. Golds shone, lighting the
tunnel of sleep. These were the colors of the North. We northerners
have a different darkness to illuminate than the South; we are folk of
little sun and use the somber yet rich colors of the Amish. We have fewer
bold colors, maybe, but our colors are equally strong.

Chapter Three

What Genius Has Old Age?

Such dark covers my northern sleep. I ask myself, "What genius has old age for accepting new conditions? What are its resources for reconciliation?"

Hans Christian Andersen had stood on Maggie and Rachel's mantel beside the family Bible. If I cut an arresting figure as first woman postmaster, Rachel thought, what of it? From my viewpoint, Maggie was a little gunpowder magazine in her earth boots, which might have been battle boots. I simply made it through my days. My back. The ice. The packed snow. Ice never melted from one end of winter to the other. My life was richly companioned. Maggie, despite her tempers, would flash home with her magic, bringing up prints from black and white to silver. All I was good for by days end was pearl diving. As I washed our dinner dishes and pans, I'd be aware of her creating—if not developing film, then sewing up vests with flowers, quilted and fiery red in words that would be equally vibrant and would flame out of the binding of my old notebooks. How could I bring myself to tell her that my writing days were over? "Make waffles, Rach," she'd say, as she wrung her hands in the doorway. I'd pull out the old black iron waffle griddle at midnight and make up a storm.

Her faded ash-rose hood hung on the peg in our hall. Beside it hung my tweed hat, a birder's hat, like those worn in Yorkshire. In those days, they said women never wore tweed. I wore tweed. Maggie used to arrive everywhere early. She wore her watch around her neck on a gold chain from her grandmother. I wore a thick watchband strapped to my wrist and was always on time.

Visualize Jo, Chel thought, my Jo, neither an old woman nor a young nun but someone with an air about her that haunted (and continues to haunt) me. In a blue cardigan, always blue, she drapes herself on our large sofa, that lumpish chesterfield that resembles a bus stop. Her glasses hang on a pearl chain about her neck. The glasses are wire-rimmed, the Ben Franklin kind we made fun of when our teachers wore them when we were brassy brash little kids with runny noses, always-runny noses. I came into the room one day laughing and crying at once.

"What's up?" I asked Jo long ago. Jo shot one eyebrow up, as was her habit. "It's Mother's ashes. The crematorium asked where to scatter them. I said wherever they pleased. Wasn't there a garden in back of the crematorium?"

"Lovely," Jo smiled, a serious smile. What I'm going through these days feels a lot like changing orders—not that I've ever taken vows. My Rubicon syndrome has set in. I am anxious with this free-floating anxiety that is pregnant: it could lead somewhere. There are many orders to life. Josephine had to master the pain of leaving Trinity despite its lure. "Doubt" Jo pointed up, is essential to faith and to love. Perhaps that is why as postal carrier, I am so often crossing the Rubicon, my back breaking with a mother lode before Yule. I knew a particular elation, an exultation as the old bell ringers let the bells peal out in perfect chime during Christmas week. I close my eyes, and once again my boots are tromping the grid of Little Norway. Here is Stonehewer's Lane. And here, Mason Street. Ironmonger's Lane winds by the Ninth Street graveyard. "Photography is my way of stopping death," she stops me short by saying. For me, it was delivering mail. Nonetheless, often on cold December days I felt I was lugging a cart of dung.

"Maybe, Jo, Maggie, and I had some terminal form of love."

"You can never tell how near the edge a person is," Jo answered.

Chel concluded her meditation. In our community Maggie and I were at the helm. Helga turned to puppet making in her forties, after working for many years as a potter. Clara makes maps; Janet Clay, who collects rose globes with flowers painted on them, is cartographer of light. Her face itself is like old fired porcelain. "No frills, many friends," Janet would say. Sarah Linen runs the pawnshop. Three gold balls were totally stilled in crystal weather. Movement was traded off for stillness. The balls now hung outside the pawnshop, which was a universe of exchange. Maggie and I learned from winters on the prairies that there's something terrible to be endured each nightfall. Life's not a bitch. Life is, rather, but an old woman narrating a tale.

Stars and stone angels filled our home; the angels were made from porous stone scraps. A wild angel would stare into northern winter twilight from a corner of the studio. Some nights we felt as though Little Norway was the town time had forgotten.

"My Aunt Cornelia told me that I was the black sheep in the family," Maggie used to say if I had a chore or a last request to give her when she was on her way out the door, camera slung over her back. She had been orphaned and was then farmed out to her Aunt Cornelia.

I now see the long railway that she wanted as something she ought to have had. As her departure approached, she kept talking of regrets: over the greenhouse, wishes canceled for the trip. I saw this as her becoming somewhat less generous until I realized that time alone was a thing Maggie had been asking for from girlhood. Ironically, despite her isolation with her Aunt Cornelia on the farm, she had never been richly alone. Retirement increased this need in her.

The last time I kissed Maggie's cheek, it was soft as butter. It is Maggith I see, riding through October woods or else streaking nude through spring snow with her red feather duster in hand. In another vignette, I see Maggie nursing a third after-dinner brandy, painting with hog-bristle brushes.

I see my life laid out: sorrow acres and contentment acres. I can see a horizontal cemetery and a vertical church with an oyster moon shining above it. Maggie used to say, "Photography is the magnet, and I am the steel."

The fish market was one of her favorite places: she loved its silver vats, wood scrubbing boards, bristle brushes, those iridescent discoveries. She liked pharmacies with tall old glass apothecary jars. When she left, she had a back like a cadet, her neck straight as an arrow. I'm kept up at night by the dowager's hump I developed over all those years spent bending over letters in the lost-letter department. I was put together wrong, slapped together. My shoulders kick up where the mail sack cut in. Maggie was carved by a careful sculptor. Margaret wore classic closures with cuffs to match her thin wrists.

Do I not know when to get out of the ring like the tin soldier in love with the paper ballerina? Ten years ago Maggie took the only photo I have of me. I have high cheekbones from my Cherokee grandmother, and my hair is chestnut and silver. I wear my long hair the old way, held up with one straight pin. My lady love she was. Maggie said my five years seniority and my size led to a kind of lording. That sounds feudal. That ruins our etching.

On a ship without a mate, the kid who slept behind the stove in the wood box in order to hear tales being told in the kitchen, I was the outside center of the circle of mother, father, aunts, and uncles. Maggie has taken on the experience of the artist in our era: exile. I did commit mothering. I'd see feverish looks climb into her cheek, such as during the bouts of double pneumonia. My mothering instinct would kick into high gear. I'd flame and bellow in a series of warnings. I could have slit my wrists for this steak.

One scene from my own girlhood returns. My mother plays the tall upright piano in our brown hall. She asks what the music sounds like.

"Sad," I say, "like an ocean."

"Is an ocean sad?" she asks.

"When it rains," I reply.

In another cameo, I am about three years old. Dolly is in bed with flu, one of the rare times we are apart. Night. I sit naked on our white bear rug, back on my heels before a roaring fire. It is snowing. I'm warm after the tub. It felt slow as molasses getting that approving look from my mother, Karyn. I direct my own film of this memory. Fade out. Blue rays. That memory is replaced by one of Maggie's angels.

"Live heart first and you'll land in a patch of trouble," says Jo. I sowed tons of energy, reaped barrows full of trials. Those first weeks with the post office were grueling. But I finally got to wear postal gray. Every night I soaked my feet in a tub of hot water, which Maggie poured boiling from the kettle. Spring lilac is what her eyes would make me think of then.

"The drabness of it all," said Maggie, when she came home slumping after her first days teaching art in our local high school. She flung her artist's portfolio on the toadstool of the sofa. Her portfolio was crammed with student drawings spilling out. "All uninspired. Those ugly yellow lamps that hang from ceilings, Chel, they make me want to weep."

I see Maggie stretched across the chesterfield, listening to Renaissance flutes from our big old RCA Victor. Wearing dusty strawberry stockings, Maggie resembles a jester, but she cries.

I see the bag of mussels.

"Look what's on our counter," she beams.

Sniffing, I pick up the bag to examine it. "Prunes," I frown, thumping it down.

"Prunes, Holy Dinah," she says, standing all of five-foot-three, arms akimbo, her cheeks turning to red flannel, wide mouth drooping. I frown back, re-examine the bag and find the dark jewel-like secret revealed.

"Sorry, love."

"I found them up here, Chel, in winter."

I was always the one who was penny-pinching, hard-wired for economy. When she bought the new lens cap she countered, "What about your new rolling pin?" I gazed with delight at my floury wooden pin hanging on the wall. Chel recalls the cookies that would roll off like postage stamps from the press. Star makers, quilt sewers, map makers, and potters—I see all these things. The future fades, the past draws me in vividly, and the horses of the past threaten to ride me away.

During those first days when Maggie was teaching, I rocked her in my arms. Both of us were sore from shoveling our drive, feet thick in snow, then piling wood. I recall Helga brought by one of her puppets one afternoon. She was lanky thing, white frost coming from her breath and almost from the puppet's head, which was nearly human in her arms.

"You look amazingly hale," Helga said

"I feel weather-beaten, moth-eaten," Chel answered.

While Helga brewed her coffee strong enough to stand on its own, I closed my eyes and picture Maggie and me with cabin fever, which hit us every spring. Beige was Mag's favorite color in homes. "Sepia," she'd laugh, shaking her head, hair falling forward from the nape of her neck.

"Maggith," I said, harking back to her Welsh roots, "you always want Tudor brown and stucco. I hate stucco."

Viewing houses always lead us into a conflict. We each groused. Hands on hips, dusted with spring light, Maggie scowled, fond of stucco. I'd protest, feeling I'd put on in the hips since I quit lugging mail sacks. Mag just hiked up her bib overalls from the straps for her defense of stucco. "I call it Withering Heights," I scoffed. The man who showed it to us was a retired airline pilot. He could look out the loft upon the sea of meadow and imagine that he was flying across the North Atlantic dotted with stars. He could imagine performing some heroic mission during war.

"How would we haul furniture up this narrow flight of stairs? With a crane?" I asked. The pilot kept pointing to the view. Did Maggith smile? Not my girl. Always shy of hurting people, still the orphaned child, she simply shuffled her feet in boots back and forth, first this foot, then that. She dug her hands deep into her pockets, twisted them around as if her hands were knives. The light shone hard on the wood, polished to alabaster at that moment.

"Maggie," I said when we got home, "a strong woman could smile some."

"Rachel," she said, "you see me one way. I'm the runt of the litter, remember? Those generous features: that wide, exceptionally mobile mouth, those large hands "Too large for a girl," Aunt Cornelia mocked.

I see Maggie and me dragging ourselves up those stairs to the house we almost bought, my back aching even then, me in my long tweed skirts. I must have looked like Gertrude Stein. The staircase had a wall along it with a row of pegs for hanging caps and jackets. Maggie, my antiquer with spring-lilac eyes. When we went down to the pilot's kitchen, he bent to remove a loaf of dark bread from the oven. We looked up at each other conspiratorially. It was the only warm thing in the house.

We first fell in love in the St. Olaf Young Women's Christian Association. Two female monks. I fell like a ton of brick for this upstart photographer with the quicksilver body and fast temper. I, who never knew I had a romantic bone in my body. I see the red flannel in her cheeks when our arguments began. I see us on a swing set outside the reference library like two kids. I see the drained white in her face when arguments died down. We had a rough go of it because we had such a damned good go. Considering the fact that the Mitford sisters met in a linen closet in England, ours was not such a zany meeting. In smocks and overalls, in earth boots and berets, she shone. What do I offer her to go for in me? Maggie was the only warm thing in the winter of our time.

Chapter Four
Gun-shy: Frozen Letter Carrier

My last telephone bill got me a bit gun-shy. All the conversations were with Sister Jo.

No skipping rope. No sound. Now that I go it alone, I think of what Jo told me: the ultimate mysticism is involved in one's choice of mate. For the mystic, the choice is God. Jo told me that she lived with the sense of the scepter. "I'm too serious, remember? I was when I was a nun," she warned, "They'd say, 'McBride, when you start going down, there's no bottom.'" That map of Ireland was written all over her face, standing out among us Norwegians. "When I was sick with amoebic dysentery," she told me, "I became the only sister to take second vows in a wheelchair. I was twenty-one. My sickness was starting to dominate my life."

She said that only last week over the phone. I listened but did not talk much, so she continued, "If the Lord is the Hound of Heaven, is He calling you to more of a relationship with others since Maggie's departure?"

"Is she?" Chel asked.

Jo laughed. She had told me often that the first separation is from the mother, the last one, death.

God spelled backward is dog. Every child probably, ashamed, shy, has made this observation. I held the magnificent picture of Jo, who was riding a hound, sleek against heaven. When traveling with a group of nuns to the missions and her carriage overturned, depositing mud all over their habits, Teresa of Avila swore: If you treat your friends like this, Lord, you don't need enemies. Jo had laughed an ironic laugh. Our two kinds of laughter—hers high, mine low and rough—rose along in night over hot brandy like untempered mares.

When Jo and I were together next, I asked her if she thought we cause disaster in our lives. I put this question to my sweet and tough, not-so-young counselor, who is gray as a dove in candlelight, gray as mole-colored suede jackets in autumn. She didn't think so. We do get into frames of mind when the earth shifts under our feet. We become accident-prone then. Long ago Jo had told me that when Harriet was gone, she had to relearn independence. This was starting to get in the way of the best she was, she said, so she went back to what she'd originally seen as prayer: a relationship.

"Relationship?" I asked. "When you love someone, you don't merely praise them. You tell them they've got the power to help you. You trust, so you make your needs known."

"Is that why you left the order?"

"It's why most of me has remained."

Harriet takes Jo for what she is, strong. I take her—or would—for what she is, a woman. The links of steel are fiery and frail. The first time I saw Jo, she was gray-eyed with a pearl tone to her skin and remarkably expressive hands, charcoal shadows falling. The first time I saw Maggie, she had sun-strained eyes, hair bleached from the sun, with a habit of throwing back her shoulders. The last time I saw her, last winter, her eyes were clear with the definition of a new need. She had been reading *The Love Songs of Ovid*, the poet in exile.

*

I wrung out the dishrag. "Maggie, you must learn to be philosophical about your mistakes. You have a long stride. The potter puts the pot into the fire to earn faith, to see its shape change. Keep fresh your memory but not your grievances. In Ovid's world humans metamorphose into stones."

Maggie had nothing romantic in her heritage. She was grave and serious; she was the powerhouse of talent, always ready to defend that but too strapped to let it loose. The angel, gagged, handcuffed, smoldered in the corner our room. I grew weary of living with an untamed angel. Last winter she still had something gaunt and Irish about her. I stare at the white December sky. I know the real stinkers in weather come after New Year. In that interstitial space, metamorphosis, I do dream. Temperatures of zero lasted for weeks while the years were gathering thickly in me. Jo grows thinner and thinner. I recall all the letters I received that had been addressed to St. Nick. Some days the pain increases in my chest; I live on codeine. Never mind. Those letters went to the dead letter office, of course. I see a sailor boy's tale, snowed-in cobbles of a northern town, winter magic of Isak Dinesen. The first time Margaret wore her hallmark bib overalls, she was in her twenties. Baggy pants of one type or another followed throughout her lifetime. Far too knowing for her own good, she photographed the human face. Lots of pockets she had; easy to slip film cans inside. We listened to war news in her room. Margaret was an art student in normal school, working for a certificate in secondary art education. It wasn't what she had wanted. Photography was her dream, but in those days, there was no way for a woman to make a career in art photography. I loved her, however, for her unattainable dream. It was the first time I'd seen ambition ignite that young woman who had eyes the color of rain. I saw a sea wind whipping her hair. She appeared alarmed.

Too private to be widely known, Rachel crawled back into bed with the hot water bottle at her back. The scene shifted. She and Maggie were cramped on Mag's narrow bed in the narrow room built by the even more closed minds of St. Olaf's college.

That was the winter, Rachel reminisces. I met a woman called Winifred, Cousin Winnie, who taught riding. Her phone bills used to make her gun-shy, but she was voluble and lived alone. Divine Justice. Maggie, who wanted to learn riding, sent me over for one lesson. Winnie raised Yorkshire terriers. Win cursed like a pirate. Even my ears burned. She was the equivalent of a male *flaneur*, a man about town, profane. I was shocked when she invited me to move in with her. I'd arrived wearing what I had: my long skirt. "Lift it up, girl," which not I but she did to reveal little underneath. I never became a rider. Horses rubbed me off on barbed wire fences or deposited me on the ground. Maggie was the wild one who took off across the iced pond. Not me with my big bones. Ovid wrote, "I feel as much a stone as the stones I sit upon ringed by water."

Rachel switched to scenes of their domestic life. She heard herself talking out things like a running debate on faith. It could be that by talking out doubts with Jo and with Maggie over the years, she has been able to see the three-hundred-sixty-degree circle of life. There was the issue of throwing away the umbrella. Maggie woke up one cold spring morning. About to go out the door to photograph, she said, "Rachel, I hate to admit it but I think I've lost my umbrella again."

"I suspect it's hereabouts somewhere, Maggie."

"Where?" Maggie threw up her hands, her mouth drooped, and her bangs hung straight above her grave gray eyes. Rachel had felt a wave of heat rise like a flame from her feet. It was as though a fire had been lit under her toes. "I think I have an idea," Rachel dived under the sofa, down on all fours. Her mind was numb. She figured she'd thrown it out about ten days ago. "You've commandeered it," Maggie would say.

"Woolworth's," Maggie smiled. Rachel hurried Maggie out the door. When she closed the door, her shoulders sagged. She slumped at the kitchen table, feeling no longer young. Maggie came home laughing. "The new one has a better handle, real leather!"

"Maggie, let's go halves."

"But why?"

Margaret frowned. Was there a new way to relate to the gods? "Did you have anything in the world to do with the disappearance of my old umbrella?" She shrugged out of her mackintosh, kicked off her black rubber boots, and laid down her camera rigging.

Rachel felt near metamorphosis or death. She stood brooding. "Remember that old German housekeeper who came while you were in Minneapolis for the opening last spring?"

"Why do you hire Germans?"

"Let me finish. You never met her. We were having that banshee wail in the middle of the night. I was thinking of Ovid in exile. I have forgiven the war in one way. You can't. She was a nice enough woman. She left her old black umbrella. She needed an umbrella. She said yours wasn't worth a hill of beans, so why not throw it out?"

"So you did."

"I did."

Maggie was stunned. Her face, however, soon opened into a broad grin. She flung her arms around Chel's neck.

"I think it's hilarious, darling."

"I don't." Rachel's face was as troubled as storm, the child in her alive, holding back tears. "I think it's unforgivable to throw away anybody's things."

"I might have been riled if you told me this morning. Let's put the cash right into our vacation tin."

Rachel's face had brightened a little as she rose to go to the red tin can. She felt strength flow back into her, moving slowly on bunioned feet in her old gray stockings. She reached for her brown purse, unclipped it, found a crumpled five, and dropped it in. "There," she turned around, "It'll take me a long time to get over this one."

This afternoon she'd gone into the hardware store on Mason Street. "Have you any rose bulbs?" It was the hour when things rippled the way a hoop trembles does when whacked. Swans in the public park went flat as though they were made of pewter. The birds floated between ice chunks. "Yes, please. Sixty watts each." He'd laughed in her face, rudely, swiftly. It was the beginning of a feeling she had that people were turning against her. The man at the hardware laughed, "I thought you meant rose bulbs for planting in earth."

She'd gone out into the sawing, river-like cold. She'd pictured Maggie storming in the door one winter afternoon just before Christmas, wearing that moth-eaten gray cardigan with the uneven black buttons. (Jo used to repair their hems, but their woolens were shot to hell, always moth-chewed no matter how carefully they were packed away. Maggie had articulated clearly that afternoon: "What I want, Rachel, is to get us way the hell out of this godforsaken northern land."

Rachel had quite simply answered: "Why, this northern land is hell, darling."

Margaret had stopped dead in her tracks, camera slung over her back, panting from exertion. Her windblown bangs shot up from her forehead making her appear nearly scalped. She resembled a small feral monk. Rachel herself had been walking on eggs.

Did the troubles come after retirement? Or did that closeness only serve to bring differences up like stars shining? Was that closeness darkness then?

"Maggie, I think it's this sudden not being rooted that makes you vulnerable." Rachel had turned back around to the wood stove to lift the black iron lids carefully. "And now that you're retired, it's especially strong. Maggie, you've always been an exile, a drifter."

The lines of faith in each other were indestructible: they had been drawn like lines in a hand. Tonight was the winter solstice, a year after Maggie's departure. Chel was the one who felt uprooted. She exemplified the old American experience: she was a storyteller (although now she narrated to herself) and a wanderer. Her old coat with the Army buttons pleased her: the shape of buttons, their cold brassiness. The thought of the rose light flooding into that sparse room would please Maggie. But black and white could capture the room best. Burleson pawed her knee when she came in. "What is it, old girl?" She thought again, soon my old bitch will be dead. She screwed the rose bulbs in their crooked sockets and sat down. She put on Bach's B minor mass, which she often listened to with Jo. All Bach's masses conclude with the words in Latin for "to the Glory of God." Rachel had sympathies for the warm passions in humans, but she herself was withdrawn. *Soli Deo Gloria.* The ash-rose footstool Maggie had bought one year on impulse rose before her eyes. She sipped brandy. It, too, had led to a bitter argument.

"It's meant for the foot of a king," Rachel had exclaimed "Or a young prince, Maggie, not two burly women." She'd turned her back on the footstool. When Harriet came over she said, "Why, it's perfectly inspired." What could Rachel have been thinking of? Harriet, with that Giacometti body and Modigliani off-center eyes, swiveled back on her hips. She'd turned to Maggie to embrace her with her long arms. As Jo was Rachel's, Harriet was Maggie's. Then with slightly mordant humor she said, "The rose footstool goes with Mozart in his more gallant moods."

*

Contretemps reached a point where Maggie said, "Rather than be hounded over land tax year after year, rather than measuring every teaspoon of sugar on the money scale, I'd like to live in a bed-sitter with a gas grate, like in England."

"What do you have in mind?"

"Rothmere House."

"That's in London."

"Precisely."

"Don't be sweeping, old bean."

Even wearing lilac, my eyes are far from violet; Maggie called them purple-brown. She was a poet in color despite her affinity for only black-and-white photography. Color was as luscious to her as chocolate fudge in the pan, warm for the licking to my tongue. My Ben Franklin glasses keep sliding down my nose. I must get a new beaded chain from the five and dime.

Burleson does not woof today. She sniffs around one of Maggie's old mole-green photography sweaters. Mag smoked Black Russians, that danger that took us both under its fragile lilac wing. Nice women didn't smoke, of course. The teal lake looks like the skin over a scar. Scars can ache as wounds do.

Rachel turned now from the rose light to look out the window where the weather was dormant, dominant iron, a dream town where iron weather reigns. She and Mag used to speculate about dream universities, dream towns.

Jo's voice haunted her. It could be high, like that of a boy soprano, or hush, sounding like a man's when she was troubled. Harriet's voice was often monotone. She could lull the community to sleep at times even with brilliant talk. The footstool, of course, had been inspired. They were too poor to own records back in those days, although Harriet was in the money. They owned no Mozart, no Bach mass. Its curved mahogany legs had been crafted with care. The footstool, though, served only to accent a conflict between Rachel and Maggie that had smoldered for years, the clash between economy and taste. Harriet nodded to each, contretemps rising like the mountain in *The Pilgrim's Progress*. It had been a moment of testing. I am a woman born of the monotony of the plains, Rachel had thought. "I bought it for your feet," Maggie had explained after shutting the door. The footstool turned out to be a favorite thing for Rachel. Eventually she bought Maggie a matching one in Dutch blue. "I notice," Jo would say to Chel these nights over the phone, "the words that come up over and over when you describe your situation are 'lonely' and 'terrified.'" The small house she bought with Maggie faced north. They lacked sun in winter. She fondly recalled cat-sitting at Lotte's house, which faced southeast. "Welcome, Maggie and Rach," the note on yellow paper had read. "Feed each cat once in a.m. and ½ tin each of food by back door in p.m. Fresh water daily. They like treats. If they come near the table while you eat, be prepared to brush them aside." The screen on the back bedroom window was makeshift but necessary to keep the cats out. The women found it easier to open and close the window by going out on the patio. They found front door keys hanging on bulletin board in the kitchen. They did, however, have to get in through the screen on the bedroom door once or twice. In freezing temperatures, the two had locked themselves out. Maggie, camera in hand, forced herself in. It was far easier to fall in love with talent than night, Rachel thought. But the sunlight had cheered them. They loathed seeing Lotte by the time she returned. The notes could have been written only yesterday. There were clean towels on the rack in back bedroom. The screen door could be opened from inside if you hit it sharply on the inner edge of the handle.

Those sharp nights of deep sleep. Burleson pawed Chel's knee. "Biscuit?" she asked the dog in her alto. Burleson's teeth were shot. Biscuits soaked in warm milk were all she could manage. Rachel rose, dragged the biscuit box over and set it between her skirted knees. At times, Maggie would moan in her sleep and say things from left field.

"Modern," she once moaned over and over in the night.

"What's modern, darling?"

She shook her awake, but Maggie had refused, "Let me get back," she sighed, like a sleeping child. At times, Chel believed that this sleep speech related to photography and touched upon the visionary. They strove like John Donne to make one little room an everywhere, Maggie left taped on the fridge door, "Gone photographing dawn."

*

I had excelled at spelling bees. This was the silver lining to the cloud of my childhood. When I learned to spell, I won bees. This morning, when I started a small fire with my magnifier (the big glass) in the sun, it burned and burned. I thought back on those spelling bees: how I burned to get each word right and finally won. Words held power for me. People like foxy Harriet make me feel strange. While the magnifying glass fire burned, I thought how new beginnings define boundaries.

"You have such a claiming presence," Maggie used to tell me.

"What does it claim?"

She turned nonverbal and shrugged. She could bring up silvery tints from the developing tray.

I find that I can plot a day around two outings: one to mail letters in morning, one to go to the hardware or mail some more letters in late afternoon. I become involved with hope when I write a letter. Maggie gave me the three-volume Harvard edition of Emily Dickinson's letters. I have found the place where hope springs. But also know where fear springs: I feel shrunken, small; I feel like a plant putting out shoots trying to root in air.

The room was suddenly plunged in cold: it broke Rachel's reverie. She went to fix the boiler, which constantly needed firing. The hired boy was callow. She was fond of him as one is of a son. Their boiler was dated 1917. She didn't want to go down to the ironworks in the freezing cold to try to dig up a new boiler four days before Christmas. How many nights could a gal warm herself with old Kate Hepburn movies on a flickering television that should have been swapped at Sarah Linen's long ago. Sarah Linen's pawnshop was like an illustrated tour of the Middle Ages. Much as Rachel loved the medieval period, she didn't want to tour it now. She phoned Sarah, who said she'd gone to church yesterday. Catholic cold. Get used to it. It was true; Chel reasoned that cathedrals are high and cold. I see Mother dragging me to church beneath the high ringing of Lutheran church bells. I could not whine; my daddy was the minister. I was schooled not to screw up my nose. My mother taught me that it's what goes on in your daily life that matters. In a child's mind it is not in church that the real reckoning occurs. True, I loved and respect him but at some distance. His sermons put me to sleep. It also put to sleep some folk I observed in the next pew, the whole interior of the church scene occurring with that luster of old veneer on bookcases, walnut and oak.

Starting the small fire in the hearth gave her a sense of company, of controlled warmth. White sun, which could warm no winter birds, was hidden, the only sun that had shone today. "Sister Jo," Chel had asked the other day, "Are there those nuns who leave their orders and go back again?"

"Rarely. Sometimes. People have the power to be transformed."

"But do not speak of people. Speak of yourself."

Were there leftover vestments of Jo's convent humility in her hesitancy to speak of herself? In understanding her small but genius part in the pageant of the universe, was she silent?

"I keep being hammered by everything that happens. I seem to be a person who cannot stay lighted." Jo saw the world lit by the great fire under the altar like the crackling fire beneath the pot on the cook stove. Thorns crackling. She had ironic ways of seeing her calling.

Rachel found comfort in daily chores. On this cold day she could not come to grips with the grief and fury in it, but she mulled over the words that Sarah Linen had worn home on a lapel pin when she returned from a recent trip to Canada: FALL IN LOVE AGAIN. Chel envisioned Maggie, nude in front of the fire in their home, just as her own mother must have admired her. I was a child with dark hair for a Norwegian. It was all about the mother falling in love with the child. I kneeled before the fire at four, at five and could feel my mother's eyes grooming me. The years have washed by. Maggie's freshly washed hair swung forward, exposing the back of her neck. I'd plant a kiss there and, startled, she'd wheel around, so I would plant one on her lips. Color would be reflected in her cheeks from the fire. Red flannel. She would kneel, heels trimly under her butt, drying her hair with a torn white towel, thorn-white. Dolly's birthday had always been my birthday until we were fifteen. Death severed us and gave me my first birthday alone. In the fairer, thinner-boned Dolly, I saw Maggie, or was it the other way around? Take it back, Death Horse, this dying. I shuddered, bitter and tall in my new shoes. Who am I? I am Rachel.

That life had been richly embroidered. The pages where as thick as a time of fairy tales. She met Margaret when Mag had barely escaped the walls of the thin red-brick orphanage. She'd mothered her. But she loved her too with a passion of many years. Some days the women formed a taciturn community; one of few words. Some days, many words wove back and forth. Jo instructed them to listen to what people say in their grief. You never know how near the edge a person is. Even around women who loved and accepted her, Kay Kendrick showed a form of desperation, of treading on thin ice, breathing a thinner air than the rest of them. Because we are born, Rachel mulled, under the sign of Saturn with what is called a melancholy cast. We got us a house with a big kitchen for me to bake bread, for Margaret to have a darkroom next to it, to give us elbow room, so we could roll up our sleeves and bake. And we certainly used elbow grease. We learned to teach each other about our childhoods. Talk functioned as touch for us then. We rehearsed those girlhoods. Few impulses were forgotten.

The past resonated with us because it is dark, mysterious, the storehouse of our memories and emotions; the box of our past is polished with a kind of rosin. I brought her the childhood I wanted for her, kneaded it, rolled it up as though I could bake it in the oven until it rose. Through those unforgotten winters, we would read aloud to each other late into the night. Mag made our candles, dipped the tallow and poured it over wicks. Lime-, jonquil-, and sap-green candles, like her tubes of pain. These hung by nails in our rooms. She rolled soaps: pale blue, stony gray like a cat's eyes. We always had a cat for her along with my sheepdog. She'd set her soaps in a jar just like our grandmothers had. We had a round glass jar of soaps in the john, which faced east and caught the morning light. The rest of our house held northern light. Maggie loved photographing our bathroom: light on porcelain.

Maggie was like a sponge, soaking up all she could. She had a button collection: wood and brass buttons from old Army and Navy greatcoats.

She'd been a WAC. I was in the WAVES. She worked in a photo lab.
Much of our affair was in fact conducted in uniform. An occasional
brush of arms in non-civilian clothing lit our fires. An erotic touch could
exist in servicewomen's garb. Up our sleeves we were laughing. I collected
stamps, she culled buttons, but both of us hated sewing.

"Tell me about silver salt," Chel would say kicking off her WAVE
shoes: black, sensible, ugly.

Maggie told me that when she was ten years old, she'd seen a man
and woman walking through the woods throwing their shadows. She
knew there was a way to gather up those shadows and put them into
the black box. She had found a way to enter the universe. She was as
sharp as mustard over this, which is why our arguments over checkbooks
hit her where she lived. They got me between the eyes too. Money and
mercy. Combine them. We were walking on eggs so thin that, like
ice, they could crack. She forgot every time where she had stashed her
checkbooks.

"They're safe," she said, pulling out linen cupboards, banging drawers.
"I can conduct my life without you, Rach, just as I did before." Her life
had been running along before, Rachel thought, so I put the checkbooks
out of my head time and again. "You are more charismatic than me,
Maggie. You'd be better at going to the bank people." The books would
turn up or she, Rachel, would explain how Maggie had misplaced them,
but they were in a safe place. Maggie's cheeks were on fire; she would
stutter over the issue. These were the requirements of love. Maggie would
spill food on a burner. It happened at least once a week. "Better than a
person getting burned," Mag would bark back. She'd stand on well-shod
feet, she who dismissed silver salt and pepper shakers as too fancy. A
paperwhite matures in a glass jar in the bathroom.

I'd barnstorm out like a paratrooper, come back recondite, bringing
some object to bury the hatchet, even though nobody ever forgets where
he or she buries the hatchet.

With simple, untrammeled dignity, I'd say time after time "our
prayer plant." Many cherished things came out of these arguments over
the bank. Like our cream lace curtains. Our plant's leaves were quite
unearthly, growing out of the more quirky demands of love. Its green
shivered and shook like a saint receiving a vision, perhaps a shaker
getting ecstasy. Mainly in evening it shook while we would turn the pages
of some book. I see it now as I set out a fresh dish of water for Burleson.
There is something about setting out a metal dish of clean water for an
animal. These frozen Minnesota nights I see us living dangerously near to
the symbol of fairy tale.

She had washed the spinach leaves. These nights were so different
from those busy years. In the post office, walking frozen streets in
winter and burning grids in summer, Chel had had dogs barking at her
stockings and imagining Jo's nearly southern voice, the music maker of
Ireland.

Talk would be touch. How enticing she and Maggie had found
Washington Square Arch in Greenwich Village.

*

It is 1939, the last year of the Dirty Thirties. They meet while war is
raging in Europe, threatening to cross the Atlantic. Or will the States
remain aloof? They are walking perhaps the last mile of peace on the
North American continent. Walking. In some ways the world appeared
to be opening. Rachel lies on her back, as flat as if in a coffin, imagining
what it must have been like to be in France the night war was declared.
They couldn't walk arm-in-arm under the arch or anywhere. In the Big
Apple as in the Windy City. They would occasionally glimpse Marianne
Moore in her Paul Revere–style tricorn black hat. A librarian, a poet,
a spinster, she summed up courage. Like Emily Dickenson, she was
devoted to her brother. New York and Amherst were as alluring as
European towns to a woman from farmland Minnesota. The women
glowed with their exposure to culture as though they were litmus paper
going through radical change or a negative exposed to the chemical
processes. Their ears burned. We were like bones lit up by a safe dose
of radiation. When we returned to Little Norway, the town was more
shrunken than ever. We came back to take up posts as civil servants:
teacher and postal worker. We were not comfortable in the town that
time had forgotten. "Do you feel caught in a treadmill?" Maggie turned,
her blue eyes darker after dinner, wringing a cloth as though she were
wringing the provincialism and poverty out of our lives. Where was the
tin soldier? Where was the snow queen? I stood on the railroad tracks as
a kid, dreaming my way into far-off places. A twin, so young I was sheared
from Dolly. Life always had a dreamlike quality for me: when delivering
mail, the sack sitting on my back, standing on a stoop, with box in hand,
ringing a doorbell, hanging on like grim death, nobody coming, only the
dog inside barking. Dogs followed me. Life kept its dreamlike tone as I
walked home through thickest snow, my mail sack as heavy as a gun.

*

Tonight she took her Joseph's-coat-of-many-colors quilt everywhere,
set it on her knees, American history written across her lap. She hauled
down the letter-writing equipment. She had a tablet of lined, block-like

paper she kept next to Hans Christian Andersen. One sip of white wine and that old dog biting the back of her heels, the hound of heaven. Or was it the angel, and was there any difference? Joy lit a nimbus around things: old iron cookware, copper kettle, skillet, forty-year-old fry pan.

Jo, too, wrote letters: in this way the women were mirror images of each other. When Harriet was out of town trying a case, Jo would commit herself over and over again to the bond shared with other humans by her careful, uphill writing. The breviary would be by her side. She'd write one letter after another to the sisters she'd left. Had she ever forsaken the world, the flesh, the devil? She was the shrewdest judge of human nature Rachel knew. I am probably in love with Jo and have been for as long as I have known her. I envision my hand tracing letters over her thin hand. The world she knew, that network of human relation in the order hasn't changed. Heart of gold, nerves of steel, our Jo.

Why and how did Maggie gradually withdraw? She began sleeping in a separate room from me—after all these years. Her war dreams began recurring. Churchill knew that the Germans had found a most effective psychological weapon in the unexploded bomb: prolonged uncertainty. The British, however, were experts in keeping cool. Did she notice that my frame of mind was like sun shining a degree less bright? The circle of the lamp felt as white as the Arctic Circle. I cannot sift the mystery from the light. When two love, much can come between them: the state, the cross, the world. I often made a crackle with my big boots on leaves in autumn when she went photographing. "Hold perfectly still!" she would command. She thought I could hold still the way the lake holds still. Where, Lord, were you, my hidden advocate? See how your daughter Rachel suffers. She went through rough years, and now with retirement this has come, this estrangement. But no one was listening.

*

Jo had written her letter to Rome, which is required when one leaves the clergy. Tonight all the echoes fell away. She had served the order for seven years before meeting Harriet at a legal conference in Denver. After ten months of fervent outside-convent-rules correspondence, she knew she wanted, indeed needed, to be free of her vows. She moved up to Harriet's town in Minnesota. Rachel, during that time, had fallen for a young woman named Margaret. She fell hell for leather. Maggie was bent on building her own darkroom. "Try color," Chel had suggested. "You are too young to block out color." Meanwhile, Jo learned that she was still young enough to welcome color back into her life. "I have tried," said Maggie. "I had ambitions to be a painter when I was younger. Now I know silver is my color, the silver that I see shooting down through trees, skies, skeletons. I can work only in black and white."

So it was that I came, thought Jo, to spend my life with Harriet.

So it was, thought Chel, I came to spend life with one of the most challenging photographers I had met. Color hadn't yet been perfected. Black and white was further along. Color could only let her down. She used to stamp her foot. I was crazy for her. That winter we met I was not gun-shy. I would spend my life, although I didn't know how, with this woman.

Chapter Five
Flames and Red Stockings

There is a saying: "red shoes, no knickers."
Two days before Christmas, Rachel counted stars. From her kitchen window she could watch them leap like flames in the sky. As she glanced to the left, she saw similar stars leap in the grate. One, two, three fill my window. They quivered like a boy through a hoop of fire. She had rinsed her old gray stockings. Six weeks before last Yule, nobody in the group knew. Only we knew; we appeared as one to the world, but we were divided. "You are a sturdy soul, Chel," Jo had told me when I made it all plain.

From the street children's piping voices came: "Christmas is coming, the goose is getting fat … ." I wear the old red quilted robe. I wear it over the mole-gray sweater with torn elbow, which I've patched with gray suede numerous times. I should be buried in it.

Chel mused. What was writ in invisible ink is deepest. I see, when I close my eyes, the bowl of mussels soaking in the fridge and cornmeal for them to spit out. My wild spirit I loved is gone. A damp dishcloth was draped on top of the dish, some salt sprinkled over that. They were bearded, scrubbed with the nailbrush. "Maggie," I cornered her in the darkroom, "Now listen, it looks mighty strange to have a cold bowl with a damp cloth on top sitting in the fridge." She answered, "Well, hell's bells, I've been up to my eyeballs in cookbooks, and one said do this." What Maggie couldn't hear was that I was holding on by my nails to a marriage, feeling a lost feeling, slowly grieving over a marriage. Mag laughed, "We need real butter," she added, "so we had better drive out today and get a good quarter pound."

"But we're down to our last hundred," I said.

"Chel," she answered, "Scrape the bottom of the barrel and you get splinters. We still have enough for gasoline. We don't have to push our old Buick Deluxe into town." Welcomed in secret by Jo but otherwise by none.

"Well then, Mag" I butted in. "How did we get so low?" I saw now the tables were turning. The Roman garrison on the hill. I was a woman almost in the pangs of childbirth.

"How did we get so low? Because you keep spending."

"Me?"

I had gone to the freezer and dug and dug, but there was no real butter, only margarine. We were lucky to get it during the war. Then we were grateful.

"Damn the war," I said. Maggie beamed, "Let's rob the tin." So we touched fingers at the metal bottom and ended up holding hands. On the ride home last night, I remembered toilet paper during war. It was scratchy. It came back to me. I am stuck at the war. That's where I fit in the groove. "You can have powdered milk in your coffee," I'd told Maggie. "Powdered milk is like cotton." We fought uphill, down dale with the stamina of soldiers, foot soldiers, infantry women. Tender at the end, I'd bring her breakfast in bed. Fresh flowers on the tray if it was spring. "Two boiled eggs, tea, and a cornflower."

"We are repaired, Chel," she would grin and wolf the egg down. She had the appetite of an eagle and the delicacy of a lark. She rarely brought my breakfast. Neither of us fetched wood and drew water anymore. Our manner differed. Always robbing our vacation tin, Maggie bought a wide-angle lens. Her joy and generosity bore it, swept it in. But the issue of sexual flames, other attractions, we rarely fought out. We knew it would lead to grief. We understood how the heart moves. We knew that a smash could light up a dark room if there was ferocity to it. Crushes or flames were borne with tolerance and calm, even tenderness toward the other's affection. Sometimes I think because we wanted our love to be inclusive, not exclusive, and we pushed ourselves to the limit.

Sometimes when it stormed, I rocked her in my arms. I rubbed her back the way she liked. "You two just get up there and boogie-woogie," Harriet said. We downed root beer and burgers on a summer evening in the car, flame flowers starting up all around the old car. Our happiness was an enviable thing. We didn't stand smothered by the shadow of crisis. Those who stand in their own shadow finally swallow pleasure. I see Kay Kendrick's musicianship and independence, luminous traits. Maggie and I viewed them with sympathy but finally decided she ruled out too much of the world with her pedantry and severity. Yet what can you do if you are born under the sign of Saturn? Both born rescuers, did we fail to rescue our love at the end?

Rachel's vision became clear. She did imagine that she piloted one of the tall-masted ships at night. Over the glory, darkness, and framed in the worlds of Hans Christian Andersen. She imagined that she was shadowboxing with God. After a brawl she would sever the last nerve Maggie had jumped upon by sitting in the rocking chair from Norway that Karyn had willed her. She could feel herself bolting back tears, could feel the bolt sliding. Maggie never knew how vulnerable Chel was to those moods. Particularly, Rachel mused, when I washed her stockings. I had promised not to, but tenderness overcame me with a shot of brandy. "Still drinking?" she'd ask with a critical eye.

"No," I lied, slipping a bit more into my glass, feeling a change creeping over me. I heard Jo whisper at those times, "It goes down so easy with you, Chel," and I would wonder whether I couldn't have been calmer, more content living my life with Jo." Maggie stomped back, "Washing my hose mothers me, and I don't want to mothered." I'd lay the wet things down over the back of some living room chair. More often I'd wash them again on the sly, enjoying lathering them, feeling that this act bore away some of my grief. Like mother Karyn, laundering, taking in wash, I poured energy into washing as I did into shoving mail into sacks. Maggie's delicate embroidered stockings came clean. It eased my loss over no longer making love. It bore away my wrath at Mother, who wore only scratchy things on her legs, which were stout and strong.

Maggie's hose came up like laughter out of the suds, burned strawberry, dusty blue, those colors one can taste on the tongue. I have a thing for feet. I liked holding her foot in my hand. Mine are a sight to scare the dead, engraved with bunions, hills from Carl Sandburg's rutabaga country. Then there was the phone. Who dare criticize her companion on the phone? Maggie was crisp, sweet but brief, as if a hot poker was burning her slowly at times. Why can't you take more time, be more kind, I thought. Why can't you find it pleasant to be inquiring, you, who are essentially kind? Now I yearn for that brevity. I long to burn a hole in people's smug lives. Where they are locked in, I am locked out.

I have the feeling Harriet is the shutting-out kind of brilliant. Ah, Maggie has a Breton sailor's hat brought back from Britain by a friend. Blue, it was, with a red pom-pom; she put it on after some of our arguments. She won. She hung it on the four-poster some nights when we felt mean. Once I left to chair a weeklong postal convention; I left in postal gray, and I came home in postal gray in an even grayer mood. The hat was off the post. Three plants had died. "They died," I said. I pinched them, probably wearing my funeral expression.

"Yes, and you better believe I watered them."

"How often."

"As often as you wrote on that chart," she pointed at the chart taped on the wall. I walked up to the chart and stared at it. "They're dead." "'Rachel," she said, "when you're tired, you can be mean." Then she halted, "When you're worn to the bone, and that's the only time."

Maggie was right: she was born with a red thumb but I with a green one. We had certain needs, which grew aged if not watered. Often there was no release except for her to leave the house. We would take a long drive or walk. She'd go out with her camera and come home docile. We labored few points. Our wombs felt empty; our bellies ached. We reached out to someone we couldn't win and withdrew like the green shells of the snail. Is this an epiphany? It is Maggie bringing the world closer in through her lens until it is all blue-green flame. She will transform it, of course, into black, white, and silver. That is my goal too: for print to make the world clear, but in my case through the posted letters that I carried. So we each bring the world in close to make it more touchable, human. Perhaps we dream that day when we all become comprehensible to one another: the Helgas, Kay Kendricks, Harriets, with all of our contradiction and mystery made clear in the light. Maybe it will be like that day when Maggie came to the old Buick Deluxe and said, "It's like small points of flame dancing on the water." I see her sitting up in bed, reading a Regency romance. She enjoyed the flair to them, the flair and blare. It was Maggie's diversion. For us love in a cold climate is the reality. We live nearly in an Arctic Circle of affections. Mugs of hot brandy and milk stand steaming at our side. The Breton sailor hat is on the post, the shawl over our backs while our arms are about each other. I see us spending hours and hours in winter in the car thinking how good it would be to have butter after all that margarine and chocolates and stockings. To have her and snow falling at once: I could not believe the joy. I can feel my own generosities change, like fluids in the body shifting. We drove past the place on Ironmonger's Lane that we'd once thought of buying. She'd keep looking back, then slip into the car, and we would drive home in silence.

Maggie and Jo represent twin balances to a scale. Maggie would often wait for the dark before dawn. Jo would say that it's darkest before dawn. "I used to fear my faith was slipping. I no longer defined faith as God. I feared that I would get stuck at the darkness that comes before dawn." But there had come a time when she said, "There is a spiritual roundness and simplicity to things for me now." Had Rachel made Jo a daughter because she could not take her as a lover? In fact Rachel herself made a retreat to the Franciscans over Jo before she met Margaret. "I would love you," Jo finally said, "for the remainder of my life." Burnt in the body. It was Jo who started the rumor than they two were founding mothers of the community. Despite her Modigliani face, her hair almost the color of champagne and pre-Raphaelite profile, Josepha had a quality of indestructibility. I saw earlier photographs of her: Jo had been a serious girl with a champagne-colored braid down her back and an Irish surname. She'd gone to Catholic schools. She grew into an even more sober young woman with her S-shaped spine and one leg shorter than the other. (Many nights I imagined that I rubbed liniment into her spine.) Her forehead was noble; it defined a thinker. She would frown from time to time, the mark of God. Spectral, marble, a bit like Dolly, a revenant, she had magnetized me through my teens, but I knew she was not of my world. She was from the Irish part of town. I must have looked prematurely ancient in high school, ham-handed, five-foot-eleven at fifteen, my spirit sought refuge in books and thoughts of becoming a reference librarian. I had inherited a very long gray skirt and pullovers from an aunt. Yes, gray was my color even in the bloom of girlhood. I was camouflaged as a mole.

When Jo came out of the convent, her back was more S-shaped than later, her leg shorter than the other by more than an inch. She was twenty-six. Her gray eyes were resolved. She gave me, Rachel recalled, *Earthly Paradise*, by Colette, when she came out of the order. She took first vows at nineteen, second vows a couple of years later. "Jo, what do you look on as evil?"

"The conscious and willful turning from God, from love."

"That it?" "For me, yes. It's open to many interpretations." From anyone but Jo religion was a back archer, but Jo came up from under. Up from those mesas of the Southwest where she'd caught the dysentery that almost killed her, where she'd trained in social work with poor Spanish-speaking women. Back to the blue, the ice-blue northern woods of her birth. But she wanted to return to the heat, where she felt her soul was burned clean, the Southwest. She exited the white cloth when I went into postal gray. We each took up our lives with our companions in Little Norway. What is the passage of time? Maggie and I had each wounds of degrees.

Rachel now heard the Doppler effect of the midnight train leaning through this American dream. Maggie could get into one of her Griselda moods and naught could get her out. Scoured by ice the world, "We are both involved with light," Jo said, always still a sister to Rachel. "We serve its secrets," she explained. She found the light darker in the United Kingdom. Even though she'd gone to England with Maggie several times, lugging lenses and rigging along, Chel felt herself to be profoundly of the American heartland. My toes are in the Mississippi, she felt, my head in the North, where Paul Bunyan went with Babe the Blue Ox putting hooves down to form the great lakes. I can strip life down. Beauty makes me nervous, yet beauty is a magnet. "A short circuit can smolder behind a wall for hours," I would warn Maggie "and we don't know until there is a big fire."

I could have helped myself, been a bit more optimistic. Why was I hard-wired to fear? Nothing nasty had happened to me in the woodshed.

Jo had chosen the Franciscan order when she was a nun. She owned little. Jo's austerities, the opposite of hemming her in, broke walls apart. "The bird has his nest, the fox his lair but the son of man has not where to lay his head." St. Francis died at age forty-three. She taped his sermon

to the birds on her wall above a plain wood crucifix. All the sisters did
this. Even now when she said the words, "The Lord," after all these years
out of the convent, Josepha said it with a bow of the head and a hushed
tone. Like all spiritual orders, hers believed in stripping life lean. They
knew how to lock back tears. Her order particularly observed that the
animals are able to become one's brothers and sisters if one gives up all
earthly things. Sister Hen. Brother Rooster. So Josepha had been brought
to her spiritual translucency. Although Rachel had marked this in Jo as a
girl, holding it her coveted secret, the thin girl with single braid the color
of change.

*

Chel imagined Jo with the jeweled eyes of a toad, an Edith Sitwell,
that head almost too large for the small uneven body. Jo had almost got
the bulging eyes, those of a fairy-tale prince, the eyes that are not eyes at
all but really gems.

What is happening to me? Rachel obsessed. Like Jo when she turned
fifty, I feel all that is solid beneath me melting. Those four walls that
protected me are coming down. To become more human? The shadow
of the past is coming into the present. Maggie said that she felt trapped
by our love. That's the other side to love. Jo instructed me that love
could be like waves of the ocean: the surface is roiled. Even though
I am without Maggie in the flesh, slowly the feeling of being all right
comes over me. "Your core is that strong," Jo smiled. "Can you still enjoy
breathing?"

"I can." We lost ourselves in what's around us. The phone may be
down and the car not running. Our heart may feel on the outs, but
somewhere despite all this we can be all right. Chel lay her strong broad
palm on Jo's back and felt how alarmingly thin Jo had become over
autumn into this winter. "The trick is to hear the voice at the other end,"
Jo had said at the door. "If you have troubles when you are young, you
think you will give them to God. But to ask him to solve your problems?
It sounds as if God is saying no thanks, but perhaps an answer comes
that is hidden."

"Perhaps not," Rachel had challenged. "Have answers come during
your lifetime?"

"Some have, other are a long time coming." Tonight driving home,
Chel observed changing views of streets. She thought about how Jo had
softened from her days as principal of St. Anne's. When she came out
of the order, she had a degree in primary education. She had taught
religious education and French in the convent. She had been made
principal at age twenty-nine, when she taught out of the convent and

broke ground in Little Norway by becoming first lay principal of the school. She was known as Little Napoleon thirty years ago at nineteen. Changing views were like changing partners, a sharp and imminent danger was contained within. Being retired was a danger. There were open desolate windy spaces in the sky two days before Christmas, unsettling even to a Midwesterner. These vacuums were cracks in the universe through which light shone. Cracked in aged red brick or breaks in breathing occurred where danger could seep in. Why fear grief? She and grief were old friends. Rarely, Chel would phone Harriet with whom she'd go to the silver screen in order to view the past rippling before them. What an improbable combination! One was a tall lawyer with frizzy gray hair and long restless hands. The other was retired postmaster, thick-set, broad-backed, with nerves of steel and a heart whose passions were never belied by her manner of breathing, which was even and calm. They would go to the movies together, yet each was always alone. Had Greta Garbo or Claudette Colbert the power to kiss and heal? Humphrey Bogart always spoke the same words at the close of *Casablanca*. Rachel went home and would read *The Art of Eating*. She liked the chapter titled "How to Be Cheerful Though Starving," which she wrote in invisible ink with her own imagination. Tonight she boiled an egg.

Whole days were spent in bed with Maggie. A single drop of brandy could be encouraging. We continued in our ragged march every day, questioning the values of survival. Life was like the pages of a huge fairy-tale book: thick black covers and thick vellum pages embroidered with ink while white ice and hoarfrost covered all things.

There is such a thing as a guest master. There was a guest master where Jo made a retreat last winter to a monastery called Westminster in northern Minnesota. Chel had come to see herself as one in a way, since it was worthy work that latched on to the flow of life: entertaining guests. This kitchen, this gray window looking out over a patch of sky, was her world. Rachel felt herself trying to become more like her ancestors as she grew older: riveting unbroken attention on them, she wanted her memory to be like the mirror.

Grandmother collected rose petals. I never saw that exact color in anything else. She kept the petals in a glass jar on a mahogany table. We were not rich: the mahogany had been brought over on the ship from Norway. We were Viking, so we sheltered our ships with curved prows in inland covers. Our spirits we sheltered in fjords, our ears nourished with *Peer Gynt*. Rachel pulled a bag of ice out of the freezer. She knew how to bang it. She hit it along the fault line. Old woman, I laugh, you carried mail sacks that weighed a half-ton and now take pride in putting soap in a glass, just as your grandmother did. But back in our thirties, it

was all different. The war was finally over in Europe. Jo's eyes, pale as in
a wimpled face, continued to meet mine. A certain acridity and warmth
combined to ignite a fire between Harriet and Maggie and me—Harriet
who turned out be our next best friend because of enigmas yet to be
untangled. Harriet was always the hunter hidden behind the screen. It
felt as though an affair beyond the eyes was almost as dangerous as living
at the limit of radiation. It led to a comprehension. We had our own
off-balance symmetry. Maggie's photographic work had already exploded
upon my eye both as relapse from the daily world and a glimpse into the
extraordinary.

"What did you like about daily mass?" I grilled Jo. "What I liked was
that we were allowed to take our lunches. We ate them after mass. What
I liked were my brothers and I broke the ice, whacking it, along the way
to mass. You know how ice breaks; there's no penance involved. "But,
Jo, don't beat about the bush. I'm asking about later, when you were a
woman. "Then," she blushed, "then I loved mass itself." In her face I saw
the tough Irish kid who was game. Now the lines are darkening about
that finely sculpted head, as though a premature cowl were being drawn
on. She has lost twenty pounds, she who can afford to lose none. She
refuses the consolation of drink except "when I'm dying I'll take some
brandy, thank you."

I used to tease Harriet that her rooms reflected the legal order of her
mind. Black suits with white scarves and shirts were her hallmark. Books
were laid at right angles to pages on her desk. Bookcases from Denmark
were neatly hung on the wall like a nest of Chinese boxes. Her books
were arranged alphabetically. I'd call her tense and lyrical. There is a
dark and vibrant life to her rooms. In her tension, squared by discipline,
exists a dash of fun. She has a blown-glass bottle with boat inside. All
else flows out from that and from her law degree. That, and her love for
Jo, whose hair is still tawny but with some white. Out from the order
of that bottle neat as scrimshaws flow the azure and green waves of a
measured existence. On the other hand, our home, Maggie's and mine,
housed a ripe disorder of back rooms filled with plants, overflowing with
books, canvases, cartons of papers, Mag's manuscript on the history
of photography, her scores of contact sheets. Harriet had the neatness
of a clipper ship. We flew in the teeth of the wind, a whole small fleet
blowing in. That was in winter.

*

In summer there would be the welter of our garden, which was
patterned after the freedom of an English garden. There is a quilt from

Lancaster County, Pennsylvania, that mirrors our garden in its graduated colors and random richness. It is Amish, sewn around 1895.

I felt like the comic relief in the trio: Harriet, Jo, and me. Margaret was always somewhat on the outside. Maggie's eyes brought to mind the undisciplined ocean. Jo's were of the jeweled toad of fairy tales. Harriet's held the wisdom I associate with certain exquisite old lizards that have lived rock and sand for centuries.

While Sister Jo would arm-wrestle with God long after her letter to Rome, she knew that after the divorce, after one is no longer in love or haunted by the person. Not that she ever told me, Rachel mused. Some tension made Jo taut as glass, and nearly as transparent. With Maggie, there would be a month-long tussle with some dilemma: lighting, framing. The vengeful angel would come down to possess our home. Now I see her in characteristic posture leaning against a young willow in spring. Now in bib overalls with long full-sleeved white blouse, in the fashion of a young male courtesan. Toward the end of our shared life—has it ever ended?—you, Maggie, would say, "My life has been a brutal contest between the dark and the light. Has the dark indeed won?"

"What do you mean?"

"It has invaded my being." I heard the words and struggled to see stone angels. I thought you would never abandon them, Maggie, but they struck in your youth and in bitter disillusionment you abandoned them. It was a moment of defeat. Saving myself at that time from the onslaught and brute power of the dark angel was rough. In your thirties, you said, "I want to think through every single symbol we are taught. Sailboat. Train. Ocean wave. Lamb. Incest. The dark bearing down of my uncle on me in the barn. Silver salts. Beaumont Newhall. Dorothea Lange. Walker Evans. Ansel Adams.

Harriet took me aback, Chel concluded, when she confided, "Rach, the number of nights we've tied one on has increased to the point where we are hungover more mornings than not.

I pull out threads unraveling from our star quilt. Harriet had her own style: when Mag was sick, Harriet brought a bouquet of five roses and stuck one in a bud vase for my study.

Rachel quit talking to Maggie and recalled how Mag used to say, "When I am young, save me from myself; when I am old, save me from the world. The baskets and furniture stood like strange, mythological birds that slept outside in the night. They stood like the stone wall that the two women had lugged stone by stone to build with four strong hands.

In the seventh jump, the faces Chel saw about her were preparing for eternity.

Chapter Six
Celibacy and Cold Water

Oatmeal sweaters of our morning. Once I stole a yellow and orange
tulip from a neighbor's yard. Maggie scolded, red feather duster flying.
It was then that I began to see our life in a series of stills. We all eat our
slice of humble pie. Had Maggie run off with someone else? We deplored
the potential tyranny of coupledom. Coupledoom. We wanted to take
life in our hands like indigo dye or undeveloped film. I see the first
violets of spring, think of Maggie's gaffing about how Queen Victoria was
fond of violet jam, so she grew lots of violets in her garden.

*

Still One: "Our Meeting"
The winter we met, Maggie haunted the library for books on Edward
Steichen and Ansel Adams. She dreamed of learning the skills necessary
to develop black-and-white photographs. She meditated upon how a
woman could stride forth and go about rafting her own dark room.
"Girls," the head librarian said as she arched her back, "don't do such
things. It isn't up their alley." We thumbed our noses at her naturally.
"Can I help?" I asked Margaret on a ladder in the stacks. She wore
brown overalls, a Breton hat, which is blue with a red pom-pom. She was
discovering multiple exposures, superimposed images. She studied in
her room at the Young Women's Christian Association, a freezing den
where she invited me for tea, where she sat cross-legged on her cot. "I feel
nervous, Chel, like when great things are about to happen."
  "What kind of great thing, Margaret?"
  "Call me Maggie," she frowned. We ended up talking a long time. I
slung a shoulder bag over my back to return reluctantly to my dorm to
study history. "Our friendship, what of that, Mag?" "I say, let's carry on."
Carry on we did. I returned to be with Maggie the next afternoon and
the next and the next.
  By the second week, sitting on our narrow bed, my legs outstretched,
my six-foot frame aching from stooping, I hear her whisper, "Gentle
giant," and wanted to lean over and kiss Margaret on the mouth. I had
never kissed a girl, or a boy for that matter, on the lips. Once or twice
I'd been held by Lars or Karl. But instead I asked, "Where will you build
the darkroom?" she shrugged, digging her fists into pockets to draw out
an empty film can. "Shot all these this morning, Chel. Early morning
is heaven." She then turned grave, as I learned she could. "I'm a loner,"
she warned, in what seemed to me a non sequitur. "I never wanted to

become a reference librarian. It was my mother's dream for me. We can no longer fulfill our mothers' dreams. We are the first generation who had to live out our own dreams among women. There is a Sweden artist, Carl Larsson, who did a painting titled "Lisbeth." I call it "Perseverance." Maggie reminded me that day of the girl of eleven in Larsson's painting. "When I was a child," she began, "one eye turned in. A patch didn't work because I kept ripping it off; I wanted the full three hundred sixty degrees of life. My balance was poor, and the patch threw it off further." She halted. "So that's my ambition: three hundred sixty degrees. What is yours?" I shrugged, "Books." There the librarian dream halted like a horse at a post, no carrot or sugar in sight. I never saw myself as an old maid in wool stockings in a long line of reference libraries: pale virgins, antique by age thirty. Maggie more and more resembled a young Ingrid Bergman: bangs, androgynous, in a thick white turtleneck. I have never wanted anyone so. Sea bitten. I thought of *Patience and Sarah*. "That's that then," she said. "I have something for you," I said. I held forth a cheese wheel I'd hid behind my back. We devoured it, laughing, and then read up on suffragists, Susan B. Anthony mainly. We didn't know what we were precisely, but we were not traditional women. We brewed tea on a hot coil and burned the tea while we kissed. The burned coil smelled. All at once, I knew I wanted to spend my life with this woman. But I did not know how: I knew this much, however: the first step was to turn her away from her goals of being a normal school teacher into being one of the first serious woman photographers of our time.

The following Sunday night we began clipping ads for rental rooms that could be converted into a darkroom. She won a student prize. Her shot was elegant, simple and plain. It exemplified the pioneer dream: to expand by fulfilling the limits of space, to transform the everyday into the light of the kingdom. Maybe it was that day long ago that the star quilt began to take shape in Margaret's imagination; eight or six or five points emerged in cloth radiating outward like a street grid, depending on the city size. I realized that Maggie was offhand because of restrained passion. I nearly fell off the cot. I nodded. I must move toward some decision.

I write without style, except for in my weekly column in the local newspaper, "Rachel's Ramblings." But this is looking back. I began that in my fifties writing mainly about houseplants. In its quirky fashion, it became a town talk column. As postmaster, I enjoyed everything about mail delivery: the flow and drama, the history letters conveyed, history and stamp collecting. "Why, I could become a letter carrier, Maggie. My back's strong!" I thumped my rear end. "I will enlist in school to work for the U.S. Postal Service." "Can a woman?" "My very dear girl, I thought we were agreed that a woman can do everything and anything.

"With will," she smiled. We locked hands on it. I would apply for postal training when we returned to Little Norway after graduation that spring. I felt taller in my stocking feet after making this decision. After rigorous training, an oral test, a practical apprenticeship, at last my first day came. I wore a postal-gray skirt, fitted jacket, and black stockings. Even back on that bed in Maggie's room, I could see the brass buttons.

It was a dismal gray the day of my initiation, and then it snowed, thickening, winding up in a blizzard when my initiation day came: October 19, 1941. War was raging in Europe and around the bend for us. Autumn was done. Winter had touched ground in Minnesota. I plaited my thick brown hair in one long braid, which I fixed up with a pin. I was twenty-seven, Maggie was twenty-two and teaching art in high school. We put a down payment on a small bungalow.

*

Still Two: "The Darkroom"

The darkroom holds the shining silver of our days to come. It holds the solution all will spring from.

The remainder of our winter at the Y, you, Maggie, explained the way you shaped a world in a photograph's frame. You told me how you wanted to translate shining colors into black a white without crushing them; you told me that in teaching photography, you could earn your living. Skeptical, I was the darkroom, slowly becoming the room of most light in our home. We were brazen to beat the band. We wrote "Just Married" on a sign and hung on the door to the bedroom, on the inside knob. Our first home was off Stonehewer's Lane. We lifted the sign from the doorknob to put in the trunk of the old black Buick Deluxe when we drove up into the northern woods and drank a bottle of wine. Celibacy and cold water were not to be our diet for long. Today, about to take the seventh jump, I walk these frozen woods and see cats plastered to windows as if the cats owned the glass. That's the way with cats. In human relations, secrecy is not good. With cats it is another pair of sleeves. Old Norway collects them: I note taffy cats in elegant old women's windows with diamond-leaded panes, gray cats in Miner's Row. I hear Janet Clay's impeccable ninety-year-old voice claim, "I only drink the first cup of tea, dear, and it must be at a rolling boil. And mugs, please. Mugs keep tea hotter, so you get more." So her cup turned into a mug, and she got the most, hottest tea. My foot struck iron as I walked home. For whom will I make a rice mold with mushrooms tonight? Cats sit philosophically in windows to remind us that endings are rarely happy. Despite my having had various sheepdogs, Mag and I were cat persons. From girlhood on I linked bouncing balls and you with spring.

57

And a vain and huffy cat was always in the wings. I liked cornhusk dolls
in autumn and in winter red wool stockings, underwear that made
our rear ends break out in a rash. But I never got the idea of a happy
ending from anything. Little Norway wouldn't be Little Norway without
its felines and the rose blossoms, which fall on gray slate gravestones,
fresh and ancient gravestones. As the old adage went: green winter, full
graveyard. No fear. All of ours are white, bitterly white.

The only person I ever let commandeer me was the nurse we hired
that winter after I scalded my arm making pudding for Maggie in our
double boiler. Angelina Henson, the hired nurse, worked her tail off
to pay hospital bills. It was in our lives a strange, unhinged time. Half
the skin on my right arm was gone from elbow to wrist. How could I
haul about mail sacks? I'd phone Maggie from the post office sometimes
at five on a winter afternoon and say, "Hey, green eyes, it's brown eyes
speaking." Or consulting the roman numerals on the schoolroom wall,
she'd phone me at lunch break, "Hey there, brown eyes, it's green eyes
here."

"Get back there in bed, my woman," barked Angelina. One step away
from melancholy always, I was a loner. Angelina had a Swedish accent so
thick you could slice it with a knife. I had no idea at the time we hired
Angelina whether the burn would leave a scar on my arm as long as a
list of complaints. Once, I had worked in a military hospital swabbing
down floors: one thing I had in surfeit was elbow grease, so I could not
believe I was cowering. A cat may look at a king, I thought now and
then. One cat down our street poses at about five each afternoon, I
swear, for admiration. Being admired is right, for he or she is somewhat
of a beauty: marble in front of cream lace, statue of a cat. Unlike Wynn
Bullock, Maggie had no money to switch cameras when her images
changed, but she experimented with the old lens held at a new angle.
Her genius was experimentation: snow gathering on the greenhouse
roof. I see snow gathering in the north again tonight. I spy it with our
ancient bird-watching glasses. Maggie would throw parties after giving
exhibits: young women photographers would take a shine to her, and I
was extremely proud of my girl. Calico cats ported diamonds on their
breasts like decimals, glistening in wooden windows when I walked with
Margaret. "Maggie, that's a perfect still for you." Sometimes I returned
home to find her painting. "A failed painter, I am," she'd throw down the
brush, "I've abandoned this dream."

The night of her exhibit there was a shooting star. "Hey, Mag," I
called, but she came a split second too late. "You might have made a
wish," I said not without bitterness. I found blue and yellow paint that
night all over our vegetable steamer. How elated I felt tromping home

through the ice those days, not loping like now but passing homes, peeking into the hardware store, Little Norway Nuts & Bolts. Today, however, so many years later, I had what Kay Kendrick calls a peak experience. Jo, who knows Latin, Greek, the names of all the angels, even in the winter of loss has had out-of-body experiences like this: I rose above myself. I saw Dolly moving toward me in a cloud of icicles, which gleamed. I saw after a valley more than a peak, a boy fooling with rope beside a red-and-blue mailbox. A constant magnet for me was mailboxes. Life lit up around him like the light, which descends around me at times in my kitchen.

Rachel was in the habit of going up to mailboxes, thumping them like old companions. "Juniper?" today a woman yelled at her dog. Chel jumped, thinking it was she, and rushed home to Burleson. Considered an eccentric by some, Rachel still thumped the odd mailbox, an old buddy. Walking home, however, her fullness of heart lessened like the air going out of a balloon. She hugged her black Zhivago coat that was missing one silver button, tighter to her bosom and kicked ice with her tall leather boots, kicked ice with a vehemence that surprised even her. Her spirits sank to slow-glowing blue embers by the time she scraped her silver skeleton key in the loose lock. Burleson dreamed over a bowl of biscuits soaked in milk. She had images of Edison stoves, tortoise stoves of her girlhood in the three-room schoolhouse. She remembered holding baked potatoes first in her right, then left palm, then both, nesting the Idaho bakers in our hands to keep them warm. She recalled how her hands were warm for loving each night whereas Maggie was more sporadic. Anytime, old girl, was Rachel's rhythm.

Rachel decided to write Maggie a letter tonight. Her stoop was so bad she could not straighten her spine no matter how hard she tried. Carefully, she drew out the pad of foolscap paper from the rolltop desk beside the fireplace. It had done her from her schooldays on. It would do for the most serious epistles. She set the floor heater on high, not wanting to burn coal or wood tonight. The heater turned a menacing red. Made in Germany. Why had she bought it? It whirred at her feet; she chewed the number-two yellow pencil and ended up with a mouthful of yellow wood. Often a letter stopped here. She found it hard to speak put her emotions into words.

Was this isolation a telling postscript to a shared life? Snow was choking the north. Harriet was out of town again. Jo, too, was alone. The wheels of the low ground slowly like golden watch wheels, the cycles of justice. Jo's life, too, was winding down. Her features, as defined as a cameo's, are sharper now. Unlike a cameo, her body bears the message energy, as Maggie's did back in college.

Outside there was a sea with great horses of white swells galloping landward onto stern promontories. How they take themselves seriously, not knowing that in a mere hundred thousand years they will lean down with a kiss and join the turn and roll forward, as white as magnolias.

Chapter Seven
Not to Die Must Have Been the Goal

*In order to survive a terrible loss, one has to become another person.
It may seem cruel, survival itself is cruel; it means leading one's thoughts
away from the person who is gone.*

—Iris Murdoch, Nuns and Soldiers

"In the beginning," Maggie said, drafting her autobiography, "intially," yanking her shoe on with the brown bone shoehorn, then flinging the shoe in the corner. "At first, photography was a hazy art that seemed it might never mature. It was green as a bayberry bush, like me— and as wicked." The belt with two brown leather buttons had come off her camel's hair coat. Rachel, scrunched up on the cot at Y, was sewing it back on. "Just think," Rachel said, "how many people file into church in this town dreaming of their Sunday dinner all the while, their ham roasting in the oven, fat dripping into the pan. What aroma must thread the sermon as the minister talks on. I often thought this during my own father's sermons. Just think, Maggie, the pews have been warmed by generations of backsides. The pews are shiny as glass."

Oh, we would laugh, at times falling off the cot with the sagging mattress. I had a poor backup camera in those days. A photographer has a way of looking at the world, which can light up or can frustrate others. Often we would go out. Chel found day ideal, but I saw a red light to the snow in trees way up high, a rose light. I'd shake my head, throwing my tawny hair into my eyes and say, "No good, old Rach. Light's too white today. It's a washed-out sky day." Sometimes I saw a sullen gray land with wet purple sodden cabbage. "It's a winner!" I'd exclaim. "Just hold on." I'd spring out of the jalopy and spend half an hour setting up the tripod in a field. Purple cabbages would translate into dark silver, rose light into gray. The pictures that turned out rarely swept me off my feet. I would harrow earth with you, Rachel. You had broad shoulders but not my slumped hips. "We are food for word, darling," you said. I figured I ought to be carrying all my own gear, not you, but you wouldn't have it. Tripod, zoom, backpack: you carried these. I carried the hamper with our lunch: ham, cheese, cider, and apples. We had found a small cabin in the northern Minnesota woods our first summer. Brown eyes and green, we worked side by side. I returned alone to that cabin last winter. The people up north claim a woman could not make through winter alone. The cold fired me with determination. Not to die must have been the goal a good deal of the time.

In spring come blossoms. Here it's winter most of the year. On days when the world is drenching, I am deaf to everything but the music, which must come with images, vision. In yellow oilskin and thick boots, I tromp into woods. "Wear Sky," I hear my lover's voice echo, bossing me down through the years, the autocrat I loved. "Wear Peach, wear Parchment." Two childless women, we gave our garments names. "Did you drink your white grape juice?" We took care over the details of our lives. I dragged you, Chel, out into woods and rain. I was a drenched rat. We both looked like sleuths on the trail of a perfect shot. We spoke a private language. Who would know that Sky was a blue smock, Peach a nightgown, Parchment a tailored shirt the color of old bone? We came to a small pond, a coin, and a penny-farthing pond.

"Perfect, Rach?"

"Shoot then?"

"Ah, if I could only get it framed." I drove my hands into my pockets, then lifted out one hand to cup the ciggy, which I knew wouldn't stay lit in the rain. Chel shrugged, feeling her weight, a cheerful martyr to photography. I wore oilskin, and the drenching made the whole thing shine. It cleansed me. She wasn't nailed. She was positively screwed to the sodden earth and felt like a tree about to sink in. Chel spoke of Sister Jo. Did Jo feel transparent, empty, clean, the mystic's goal?

O magnum mysterium!

How do you think Ansel Adams created? Or Walker Evans? Or Imogen Cunningham? I had no idea. Chel was soaked to the bone. She met me in the car and told me to get on with it. I did get on with it, my head at least shielded by the tarpaulin over the camera. Wearing an odd yellow slicker hat, Chel looked old, with a prime minister's stoop and an awareness of irony. We got home. She took a towel and rubbed my short hair dry. "Now tell me the story of silver salts." she said.

*

Rachel lit up a cigarette tonight in the freeze, almost seventy years of age, igniting the weed against her will.

I saw that out of the hollow of her girlhood grief and loss Maggie carved photography, the safe place. I saw this the way I have always been able to see Dolly going down through the water or up earlier through stages of growth with me. Maggie called me a historical vignette, dazzling with wit. I feel like a burned out ember. What would Dolly have resembled in a windbreaker strolling along with me at age sixteen, nineteen, and twenty-one? Would we have been mirror images: tall, ash-brown hair, hazel eyes. When Maggie relented from efforts of her art, what then? Profound letdown. Time and again she would explain to me

that black and white has a spiritual quality. Color work angered her:
black and white was more difficult. Driving past fruit stands in autumnal
Minnesota she would be struck by lemony light or copper hitting fruit.
"No. Can't be done. I'm battling my way into a fresh vision." She told
me about silver tints slowly, patiently, how they began. The silvers in
the needlepoint ivy, which was flourishing, magnetized her. The silvers
crouched in the plant could leap forth from the chemicals in the pan.
Did Chel see? My mother pictures a woman in brown derby riding on
blown silk toward the sun when she was close to death. Her woman went
bolting like a shot clear through death. She was stronger, that rider, than
geographies and could outstrip a horse like death with a horse more
slender.

When looking closely at faces, Maggie felt she was invading privacy
but learning about openness and close-heartedness. The way people laced
their shoes and closed their knapsacks in rooms reflected who they were.
She was visiting reflected cares and character. Maggie wore tight-laced
mountain boots for backpacking, as photographers did. They needed
them as they needed their many pockets. As children we learned about
the physical world in Monteith's *First Lessons in Geography.*

> *What is geography?*
> *A description of earth's surface.*
> *What is earth?*
> *The planet or heavenly body on which we live.*
> *What is the shape of the earth?*

Round like a ball. That was the view from 1884. "Some day," my
Maggie said, "I will do a series called 'geographies,' when I mature as a
photographer."

And she did.

I see fear in the woman in the mirror and turn from her heavy
resemblance to Canadian painter Emily Carr, who when old and
eccentric wheeled a monkey in a perambulator through the streets of
Victoria, British Columbia, then became a landlady in *The House of All
Sorts*, bitter and poverty stricken. I light a match. Will I illuminate a gray
house mouse on the floorboard near our wainscotting? One lives, and life
gains a patina like bloom on old copper, a moss like that which covers
the forest floor. That floor is both velvet and scarred. Why and how
could Maggie's ship-like face appear forever young and my weather-beaten
one forever old?

> *What is a map?*
> *A picture of the whole or part of the earth's surface.*
> *What are the directions on a map?*

We live toward the top, crossing the boundary. I reach out my arms like the arresting owl.

In what direction from the center of the picture is the island?
North.

It is the island I am going toward, the island where we shove aside the trivial and live deep down. I want my fingers on a pulse. Volcano Bay. "Yes," she said Rach. "Some day I will do a photograph that captures geography as it is for me. Heartland, tongue, and temper. That's one promise I'm keeping." I saw the picture on the wall and knew you'd keep your promise. The copper skillet is yet to be done. You promised you'd get me one, the French kind, for my cooking. Sure as the Lord made little green apples, with your first big sale of prints, you bought me that. Good for you, Maggie. You distinguished promises you'd keep from less serious ones.

"When I was in the convent," Sister Jo told me, "I used to sit on the fire escape, where it was peaceful, and, with a rosary hanging in cupped hands, pray, "Father, keep my faith from slipping."

All of me has slipped. Maggie held her own cross of hand-hewn wood. She aimed to discipline excess from art. She pointed to Dorothea Lange. "Chel, where is that moon?" A new moon had been predicted in *The Old Farmer's Almanac*, and she had a whole series in mind to shoot when it rose over town. We had a struggling girlhood, both of us, constantly dreaming of some town draped in moonlight—like the Cumberland Gap in sun or better yet one of Hans Christian Andersen's towns in silverpoint.

Outside it was snowing again. It was better for you to leave the party before the host started flicking the lights on and off. Inside the doctor's waiting room. "If I were an artist, I'd use a quick nervous stiletto to draw it." You were a clotheshorse, Maggie. So was Jo, so long-waisted, so slim. The last thing you cared about, however, was clothing. In the doctor's waiting room, when you were twenty-seven, I counted twigs in the black and whites Maggie had bartered. The lump in your neck, Jo, turned out to be a swollen gland, not Hodgkin's. I can still see the waiting room, every detail engraved in my memory. It grows dark, brown outside and in. The winter street is reflective as glass. The room is filled with lamps, overcoats, magazines, and black ashes curling out of ashtrays. The waiting rooms of childhood—the dentist, the eye doctor—where our many mothers took us, Dolly and me. Dark, darker, darkest. I counted overcoats. I counted beads in the silver lamp chain—all lamps since the war seem to have had beaded chains. Kids of hideouts, we knew it wise to count numerals as night fell over our houses and towns. It halted panic.

More magazines: *Look, Life, Fortune.* Aunt Cornelia would take us to the dentist and wait in winter as world grew dark as a dot early, the room dense with grown-ups.

Two years ago, Josepha, the doctor came out with, "It's benign."

Canada, she explained, was colder than Minnesota in the winter she was ten. Probably not, but what had one to do with other? She curled up like a cat, pulling her long secondhand sweater down over her hips. "I need a sponsor, Chel. I see photographs in everything: in a moose, in a filling station." I told her we had been reading Elizabeth Bishop. "When my uncle drove me up into Canada, I found the cold brighter, more edge and bite to the light. At Lake Champlain, the border guards jumping out at night with flares reminded me of war. The silver surrounded everything: the dark bird on his branch has it. She explained, "The pitchers in the bathhouse spoke of the utility of life and life's design."

Maggie worked as Jo did, with the dedication of the Catholic or the Jew. She had that fiery disciplined drive, devotion. Maggie was entering that personal language through which she speaks to folk through her images. She remained rooted in it. For her, it was quotidian, straight as honest speech. A vision, which went straight like an arrow, drove her. She scraped off the superficial like ice from a windowpane or paint on a palette knife from a canvas. It had to be erased. She'd keep a vigil. She would slip out every hour armed with lens and tripod, like a sentry. Keeping a vigil for the extraordinary, she was alert as a wild animal is for sounds. "It's out! It is a fat satin circle of fire," she exclaimed after I'd dozed off. The moon indeed was a fiery circle of red satin, bright as a girl wears to her first ball. I ground sleep out of my eyes with my fists. We slipped out with boots and sweaters over nightclothes with quilted down vests, Maggie photographed the moon twenty, thirty times that December. Back in the warmth we would smoke up a storm, then down a hip flask of brandy. (Always we kept a Mickey in the purse we took.) Then we'd sleep in until ten, skipping classes, incurring the wrath of the principal. Salad days, days when I never did learn much about silver tints, silver gelatins, glass plate negatives. I learned other things. I saw the fierce profile of my own mother in Maggie. I saw that the great hollow carved out by her childhood had also carved the cave with icicles and where wild flowers sprang.

"If I had a daughter ..." Maggie, would begin.

"You'd be stern but not like Aunt Cornelia."

"No, not like Cornelia at all."

"Not like the old saddlebacks who pretend to teach art?"

"No. Unlike them, I'd be loving.

*

I said this and thought about the time Sister Jo told me, "I gave up smoking before I went into the convent." Last winter, after Maggie's departure, I suggested that Jo make a retreat with me. "It would take courage of me to go to the Catholic retreat here." Then she paused, "But courage is a by-product of love." There would be things there she'd rather forget, others she'd enjoy, like quiet meals, pottery class, long walks together. We were both grieving. But Maggie ... There was a world indeed before the war. She was developing spontaneous brushwork, experimenting with soapstone, Japanese black-on-white painting. Three years out of college her first exhibition with titles of prints "Three Musketeers," "Elf Pool," and "Blue Study." The town's women of means, like Mrs. Ridgway Carlson, Mrs. Pearl Matlock, Miss Esther Fortson, and Miss Carla Avers, bought her prints. Dr. and Mrs. Birmacombe bought twenty prints all at once. Margaret sought to rescue townsfolk from the yoke of tradition. They fought her vision because they were not ready for it. She has seen that the silence women toiled in was a form of heroism, realism. She would break the bondage with her lens. If you had been born a writer, Mag, you'd have written until the last light was in the sky. You had a Belgian woman's love for flowers. You were paralyzed by praise. It became a sort of palsy with you, set you shivering. The usual things were said about its being "bold for a woman."

*

> *Fudge! Fudge! Call the judge, Mama's got a newborn baby.*
> *Wrap him up in tissue paper*
> *Throw him down the elevator*
> *First floor miss ...*

The date is 1933. The rope thumped the dirt playground. It was not a time when one was spoiled for choice. The intensity of the child in relation to her environment was heightened by the Depression.

Not to die always seemed a viable goal. Tonight outside in Little Norway, the wind bent the trees back to earth like the torture of bending nails. It threw over potted trees out back, wrecked weeds. Chel bent her ear to the pillow; she feared hearing that guest curator, the wind "Chel, you know I believe in your questionings," Jo had said about making the retreat together. "Then will you not come to the monastery with me?" "No," the light voice answered, "Not quite right. My love sings high, I sing low." We did not make the retreat after all. We ordered in Chinese food and killed a bottle of white. We made a mess of twenty bottles. The classroom and postal system brought forward from the Depression into the 1950s were mainstays of inspiration. When the whole community, the mother of us all, seemed at odds, I kept us going. Keep me, Lord, from being the keeper of too many. If I had had a daughter, she'd be northern. She'd be forced to confront roofs of blank white against a stone-gray sky. And light perpetual goes the requiem for the dead. Photographers, too, search for maximum light. Perhaps my daughter would be a twin; it skips generations. Feverish secrets stir beneath the ordinary surface of a small town but that waking up New Year's Day saying "rabbit, rabbit, rabbit" and turning around three times, that feverish excitement I'd share with her at all times. If I had had a daughter, she would have been my passion. She would not be so strapped that she'd have to save pennies to buy oil paints and then paint by the light of the moon or a red-flickering oil lantern. These days only the wind comes through the mail slot, brass with tongue. These are white, cold virginal mornings.

Nineteen, I am watching the full moon. It is white as milk, and it takes as lover no man, no woman. I am midwestern, American-Norwegian, second-generation Lutheran. I will be buried by the main church, the small one at the foot of the hill in a forgotten town, a lost spirit buried under the moon. It is 1941.

"You never told me about silver gelatins." "But look at my titles: they say it all: "Road to Angels, "Angels Getaway," "Horse Fair," "View from Front Street," "Fire at the Barn." The photographs won prizes. "Open Shore I" and "Open Shore II" were their titles.

From the photograph "Horse Fair," I got her nickname, Tal. That was the name of the horse we bet on: he didn't win, Taliesin. "The mirror has a memory; so do I," she'd say. "Maggie, give a course in history of photography!" We have a friend, Cameron, who used to say things become more crystalline as much detail is gradually sheared away. Maggie used to fret over the lack of crystalline in the day. We enact a courtship dance throughout our lives. The pleasures of seduction, richness, and folly kick up dust like peacocks with their vivid tails. Deep down I believe that if our mothers had conveyed early love to us, we are able to endure, able to enact this dance. Some will argue with me. A glass of sacramental wine reflects the world upside-down. For a long while I've been taking medications to make me sleep. Even then there are my dreams. "Chel," Jo answered, "probably for a longer while I have been taking things for pain. First I am high. Night after night I got no sleep until morning, when the first bird sang. Harriet was gone. I felt the dark before dawn and didn't get stuck at the dark as I feared when I was young." The love that lets go. We are both in the same position, Josepha. Why did you not give up smoking? True, you looked handsome with a cigarette, swift and smashing, in a trouser role. "To enter the convent," you could answer, "I did." But you no longer acted obediently when you got out.

Chapter Eight
Lars

I was sixteen. To outsiders Lars would have been a perversion, my cousin bearing down upon me nude. To Maggie he was. But to me he was pity sculpted, with heavy wooden hands. After all, he was delayed. Pity he was sculpted with the sculptor's nearly careless and deep thumb gauge; what emerged was a gray clay figure with eyes. Lars was an ordinary person caught in a trapped mind and in an extraordinary moment. In my sixteen-year-old breath, I understood. I never gave up on him. There was naught to forgive, yet I beat back his advances as though I were beating back a forest fire.

I kept the act from Maggie.

In spring, when the trees are knocking themselves out knobbing, I'd wrap a long scarf round her neck twice, she laughing, because she took chills and April could see snow where we are.

I'd best take care. There was that time when I took a slide on ice: all that saved me was three bags of extra-large potato chips. Being ambidextrous has its advantages and disadvantages: knitting with the boys, I dropped more stitches than I purled. Singing my name with a broken arm, I came out ahead.

Jo taught me that we often get ashes for Easter. One day before Christmas, I see Maggie with her kicky brass bright boots. The day is crystalline. Helga plays her alto recorder to announce her arrival. More lilting than her soprano recorder, it also has a more medieval sound. Since the car is still on the fritz, she comes to fetch me for carols at the church down the hill. I have roasted two ducks on a spit. During the war, *The Settlement Cook Book* was our standby. The meal after carols is a glowing mosaic: one ex-nun and her lawyer partner, Helga, puppet maker, Janet Clay, antiquarian. We miss Sarah Linen. Neighborhood kids thread in and out for goodies as they careen, chasing after the ducks: Gretchens and Ingrids, Karls and Gunillas, and tow-headed Johnnys come. "I've decided," says Helga, "that the grand finale to my career as puppet maker won't be for kids. It is a passion play, close to medieval miracle plays." We fell silent. We knew the suffering and rough edges. Sarah Linen left a vacant chair, for she was down South visiting an aunt in New Orleans, the perfect place for her. Her aunt lived in the French Quarter, a dweller with grillwork and jazz. They'd do a bar crawl with residents of the Quarter and get snockered. I thought about Lars, our sixteen-year-old hired hand who was so tall that his head scraped the ceiling. People didn't mention Maggie. Last year her absence felt temporary, but not now. There was a labored silence when we came to the toast. Sister Jo, however, added at the end of the rather long toast, "And to Maggie," whence we bowed and fell to. Helga embraced me longest at the door. Hers is a thin, dynamic face, by turns troubled and enlightened by laughter. She suddenly looked almost young again. Was it the sherry that put such blood in her cheek? Alto recorder in hip pocket, she pulled it out, behaving fey, and played. I wanted to hold her in my arms like a mother or sister binding up the wounds of the year. We are almost a generation apart. Helga, with her broad shoulders, was once an Olympic swimmer. We had laughed over her being locked in a root cellar in England. She'd been locked in with the head bobby. Tonight she had a lot of eggnog laced with rum.

Closing my eyes, I can see the circuit flowing again, the carol book with faded drawings done for some child of long ago. With a Viking courage that fed us with our mother's milk, were we daughters of Leif Erickson, *Peer Gynt*, the fjords? We became second-generation Americans, pioneers, women who chose women. "Remember how we used to hide our love collections," we had spoofed at supper, "when our in-laws came? Maggie, I see you in my mind's eye out in the first real blizzard of the year. You have taken your old bayonet mount, the heavy one with the screw. Before my second eye opens, you've bolted out into that world that you adore. You wolf the ham slice on toast, gulp coffee. Bang goes the door. I glory in my hours alone. Different now. Irony galls: in late day you come home with the highest coloring, ravenous, seeming extra young. You've shot four rolls. Your eyes, though, are blue-glowing coals. I run a hot tub. You go in and come out another color, lie flat on your back breathing hard, camera and bayonet mount still icy.

Green eyes. Why were Dolly and I born with nearly brown eyes? Some people claim my eyes in a certain light are hazel. I've heard much about the mystic relation between twins. It's true. I can say so from the horse's mouth, although I was always the quirky one. While Dolly was alive, I seemed to have more bone mass, more blood in my body, could do anything, climb any mountain, dream any dream. When she died, the earth was taken like a carpet from under my feet. Do the newly dead polish their halos?

Now that Christmas is past, I sleep away my afternoons. That the old cannot walk that last mile for love is said by some, but what of the mothers who sat up all night nursing our earaches, our sore teeth? Karyn did this for the three who lived, as she prayed silently over the cradles of the three who did not. I'm convinced that a greater love can burn, does burn, in the breast of the old than it does in the young or midlife person. It scorches fine, thin flesh as though purifying it to let the light

shine. I can see the India rubber ball that we bounced taking the seventh
jump over that ashen brick playground in autumn, and the school
became bleaker yet in winter. Now I can hear scissors cutting paper.
I hear the books I wrapped Christmas Eve with Karyn and later with
Maggie, the incredible sound of chocolate being bitten. We were reared
to believe that we each have a table set in the wilderness. We were reared
from the time we were knee-high to a grasshopper to believe that we
must find our own place in that wilderness and nourish ourselves when
the rogue wave comes along. I think my slate has been polished white
by the salt crystals and the sands of time to reflect cold sky winter. On
Boxing Day, Maggie and I carried on the British tradition. I haven't slept
in nights. Tomorrow's church bells begin to peal, I see the porcelain cup
with the broken handle that Karyn gave me when I was seven. She gave
Dolly an identical one, lovely things from Finland. The cups had pictures
of children taking tea with jam. Karyn was able to see her children in
prairie winters even as enchanting. We seemed to parallel these children
on the cups in far-off Finland taking their tea with bread and jam. In my
seventieth year I wake crying, "Mama!" as I must have when a small girl.
Now church bells do come and wash over me. I climb out of our tall bed
and stand in the wash of sound, bathed clean. I think before she left,
Maggie gave me her eyes with which to see.

Chapter Nine
The Lack of Crystalline

I see this life of mine, letter-carrying, unfolding in the flatlands like
Billy the Kid. I think of all the secrets I must have toted: birth notices,
death notices, marriage announcements. I was harbinger of so much.
Mother Karyn told me when I was an awkward, oversize girl that if I only
kept calm and counted to seven, I would not trip and miss the rope. I
must catch the seventh jump because the seventh jump is lucky. There
are, after all, seven days in the week and the Sabbath comes on the
seventh.

In three days I shall go on the bird-watching hike in Brockson ark. Icy
spikes are forming on windows. I shall take the bird glasses. It is a severe
sky.

Five a.m. It will remind me of Maggie's tapestry made of seven colors
of gray: sparrow, wren, ostrich, heron, sandpiper, quail, and snowy owl.
Seven jumps of thread color. There is a temptation, turning into desire,
to go on and relive Margaret's life and mine while the wintry sun rises:
between Christmas and New Year has always been a time to sort out,
gather in, recollect, to sweep and carry out the bucket of ashes.

Six a.m. Put the kettle on.

I squint as the kettle comes to roiling boil. In England, in a bloom of
steam, I saw bright parasols of women passing in rain and felt that those
people dwelled on another planet.

Here comes the sun: fiery red, a furnace. The first bird calls pierce
the frozen air the day after Christmas. In Little Norway the sky bears
down. In her younger days, Harriet was so thin that all she had to do was
turn sideways and stick out her tongue and you'd take her for a done-up
zipper. She has an aureole of gray hair about her thin, tense face. After
Christmas Helga practices squeezing lacrosse balls to strengthen her
hands; her puppet heads gain in humanity, wisdom, amusement. When
you grow up in a family where your father is a writer, she teaches me,
you become a quiet person. I can recall the smell of the Dutch blend of
father's pipe. I remember the elegance of his long hands, which I have
inherited. I can smell the vanilla and butterscotch of his study, with a
college yearbook on the oak side table, the Bible, the breviary, the church
news, and piles and piles of books, stacks of papers everywhere. Religion
was no psychic wound with him: there was a chill to religion. There was
the lingering warmth of fine old varnish on desks.

Janet Clay must be rising now, the first red of winter sun firing her
face, brewing her first pot of tea, making sure that it goes into her mug of

bone china. Helga must be with her puppets, proving to herself the even harder truth and strength of the human effigy. There is pig and peasant in us all, Rachel concludes. The children raid the larder for leftover stuffing from the goose, for pastries, for thick plum pudding. She glanced up to prints of snowy owls in rest, which she'd bought two months ago at an auction. I never looked on her or on anyone as my savior. Finally, when I asked Jo last week, "How are you really?" she answered, "I'm having a rough go of it."

"So am I, sister, so am I." Two fiery copper wires lit up by rain, we turned electrical during those moments. Bring the cold birds, make sandwiches now with stuffing, to the Nevelsons, the Brocks, and the Andersons. "Patience is no penitence," said Jo, who did not mouth pious platitudes, although she admitted that she probably taught with too authoritarian a tone those years in the convent.

To be a rugged male child was once her dream, for it seemed to allow all freedoms. A boy! One of the stoic French boys, hair blown back like black feathers from his brow, coal hair, a thirteen-year-old brain filled with imagination but not yet dark, disturbing demons. You have a spine, her mother warned, so straighten up and use it! She had these thoughts as cold cracked her backbone as if the vertebrae were knuckles. I never made a blind retreat toward Christ. In inky darkness I realized that Sister Jo was holding my hand. I put an arm across her back. "Forgive me, I know among the sisters, such acts as love occur." The boxes were all wrapped now, including the cold bird.

*

Maggie looked down at her hands, hamstrung, and smiled on them. "Strong," she said "from pulling cows' udders." As Rachel walked into the cold morning with the boxes of cold bird she felt alarmed, alien. She had forged a way to live against the grain, but now she felt coming towards her a new and frightening hostility from the closed windows and doors of the town, as if this wasn't the town she'd lived in most of her life. It was surreal with even a tinge of horror. Was it because of the night she had lived through one step ahead of despair, melancholy: Had she recently had the sort of reflections, brandy-induced to be sure, that led her to distort reality? Did something powerful have a grip on her, changing her subtly from trusting, generous, and connected to closed and mistrustful? Gossip in her own head turned into character assassination. She could sum up this dread in one word: calumny. False accusation, defamation. Her blood ran thin and cold. But I, Rachel, have done nothing wrong. I have been abandoned. There is a taint to being abandoned, but I have done nothing wrong. She remembered the Japanese dictum, "To die with honor when you can no longer live with honor."

*

Sarah Linen was an enigma, an Ishmael, always an outsider among Little Norway's community of women. Call her a unicorn. A powerhouse, she stood five-foot-three, one hundred pounds wringing wet, brassy but warm-hearted. A woman to run a bordello in New Orleans. In pumps and bangle earrings from the five and dime, Sarah bartered at her pawnshop all day. A late bloomer. A closet lesbian, she'd been married, had four kids. She framed a world for the community of women. Janet Clay framed a world as well but in tints more subtle: rose, mauve, beige, blond.

When Kay Kendrick came into a room, music was at her heels, a fine hound on a thin silver chain, a greyhound from a Flemish painting. Kay was demanding in her spiritual austerities. When Kay had briefly lived under their roof, there had been a hint of threat in the air. One affection can threaten another.

Rachel walked along the deserted streets, boxed birds in hand, thinking these things. Air stung with ozone. Hard edges to things hurt the eyes. It stunned her to see too much, as if glass were cutting her eyeball. Rachel found herself quarrelsome. Maggith and I were May and December, a classic pair. Nothing could come between us more than the balance of the natural year could be upset. I go home to thumb through my stamp collection after delivering these cold birds and dressing. Pretty soon I won't feel so low. I will be reading *London War Notes*.

As she came in the door, the phone was ringing. It was Sarah Linen, "Home so soon?" Rachel asked her. "I returned early. I'm battling my gas man. He's intrigued with my Wedgwood made many years ago in England. He put his whole body in the oven, Rachel, and his weight broke the door. Can you imagine?" Rachel indeed found it hard to imagine. Sarah's brassy voice came over the line. "It has to be mended. But, old bean, what's worse is that I was supposed to have died last Sunday," Rachel laughed. "Seriously, a neighbor concocted a rumor that I died Sunday night. She met Rachel with tears in her eyes and said 'Sarah Linen died Sunday night.' Must've dreamed about me, or seen an apparition. She hasn't been eating, you know. When you stop eating, you stop feeding your brain. Sarah, get off the phone and come on over. I need your company." Sarah did come, with a bottle of Jim Beam.

When Jo dies, I think she won't be in some dark night of the soul but in some morning the likes of which most of us never know. When

the world flowed past Maggie and me in colors of iron, Maggith held
her camera. "Iron rain" she said. Iron water and indeed iron oxygen, if
such things were possible, flowed past factories in the spring thaw, past
bricked-up linen mills, with streams that run before them to power mills.
"Gospel" and "Epistle" were our names for the two factories that flanked
First Lutheran Church when we were kids. When Maggith was one week
out of bed after a bout of flu, she stood on a steep rock photographing
some twigs she believed were being trapped by a stream, forming an
island. I thought she'd fall backward in the stiff wind. I sat behind the
dashboard thinking words I can't repeat. Her hat lifted on her head like
a parachute shimmering in wind. How mortal. "Gone photographing
dawn." That was my girl.

*

"What are you giving up for Lent this year?"
"Chess."
"Yes, Jo," I laughed, "for you that would be sacrifice."
"Conversion. It's a king's game, royalty."
A brand new year and dressed in mourning clothes: gray chiffon,
white rain. December and May, Maggie and I.
Come and kiss me, sweet and twenty, youth's a thing that will not endure.
Where is the door John promises opens? The mirror that reflects?
Momentary death is what this could be. "*Bisous* de France," Maggie
would stand on tiptoe and kiss the back of my neck on New Year's Day,
when traditionally I'd start up a vegetable soup. What's more provident
than to fill the home with bouquet of celery, onion, tomato, potato, and
beans simmering on the first day of the year.
On rare occasions I baked black-and-white chess cake. I feel old as
December all year now, or most of it, in my Navy pea jacket, brown
gloves, and shoes tromping about our garden in the muck of spring. One
year we decided to raise chickens. We weren't allowed a rooster within
town limits. With my collapsible bike leaned up against the weathered
tool shed and Maggie's collapsible umbrella by the kitchen door, we were
well armed. Until Pamela came.
When Pamela came, Harriet rolled up her sleeves and scrubbed Jo
and Harriet's ramshackle house from top to bottom, flint to cinders.
"Harriet is up to her eyeballs in cases," Jo would say, "and when it comes
to housekeeping I'm ham-handed." I'd polish off the work, bake some
bread to get them started.
In December I went to bed with my glasses on. Maggith slept with
them on the bedside table. "I can't find them, like my umbrella," she said
in dawn. "Well, never mind. Her face looked too thin, eyes frightened. I

saw the map of Ulster flash across them as though I'd had an apparition. I scanned cupboards, but there was only plum jam. The glasses were tortoise shell, forty bucks, her new big reading ones. "Well, Mag," I'd say, "don't be surprised if we wake to crunching glass." In morning she uncovered her glasses while turning back the predominantly blue star quilt, the lenses shining like bright ponds.

Networks of affection shone silk bright against the barren New Year's air. I thought of Stockard and Cam, who met in college as roommates. It wasn't long before each realized her affection went far beyond wish for verbal combat and companionship. The requirements of love were in play: humor, wit, and intelligence. Yes, but Cam's face grew more readable to Stockard with the hours, and she felt richly companioned in new ways. The dean of women, making a routine check of the door one night, flung the door open upon Stockard and Cam. Both girls were put on probation, threatening letters having been mailed home. They were inseparable. Both became elementary school teachers, famous friends to other dorm mates. One summer, motoring up into the high woods behind Little Norway, they had a head-on collision with a logging truck. Killed mystically entwined, they met death as romantic lovers would wish to. "There is no dark island on earth, no hidden corner nor nook of the human soul which is God-forsaken." Those were Jo's words, but as I enter my final years of life, I reach for May. New Year's. A long-overdue library book falls off a shelf. The phone is astoundingly silent. One can almost hear the earth turn.

"My fears," Rachel began two days into the new year, seated before the fire with Sister Jo, each with glass in hand, back to the flames.

"Do you want to talk?"

It was a strange moment. The two had walked home from Little Norway Public Library, each with fresh stack of mysteries under her arm. Jo read historical mysteries, Josephine Tey's *The Daughter of Time* and Dorothy L. Sayers's *Gaudy Night,* until, if she lay on her back, the leaves of the book tumbled into her face, soft as velvet the worn pages were. Chel in flowing cape liked that she resembled Sherlock Holmes. Was Maggie not Watson with the fine spy glass? She delved into history, *London War Notes* and *Black Lamb and Grey Falcon* by Rebecca West; she let no account of World War II get past her. These authors were women who sharpened vision with the mind's lens. Looking acutely at medieval puppet plays, Helga, too, honed her pen on these visions: the play enacted vision. Rachel stooped; walking was becoming markedly slower for Jo, although she never betrayed how hard it was. That early evening, returning from the library, her spinal deformity was noticeable to Chel, more than at other times. Jo's load of books was particularly ambitious.

"To make concrete a fear," Jo had spoken as though continuing internal dialogue, "That's the trick. The unknown is the worst demon of all." Rachel felt tender toward Jo. They went along together. What a pair, what a contrast: Sherlock in flowing postal gray, ex-religious in thin bones. In the habit of silence punctuated with words, heads bent, Jo said, "Love is time-consuming. I ruffle the waters." These words like birds were cold, wintry, crystallized, framing Jo, Josepha, Josephine, so many names Chel had for her. "Let me bank the fire," Rachel said with kindness, shoving the heavy door in. How thin Jo had become, like a shrunken cast-iron bell.

What a bitch life is. "Shall I stay the night?" Chel asked. "I, too, ruffle waters." She stayed, slept in one of Harriet's old nightgowns: they roared at how tight it was. Chel had had the thought this night, as she had before, to slip into bed beside Jo. She thought of the Chinese saying: an old person will take a child to bed with him, with her. Instead she stood in door, "What a light you have about you, like a Quaker." Black, moonless, it proved a hard night for sleep.

Sarah Linen phoned to say she was in deep trouble over her gas man. "I'm under the table, old bean."

"Be over," Rachel reassured her. One week into the new year, had she kept her one resolution: to totally let go any lording it over anyone? No, she chewed yellow pencil, digested more lead and yellow paint than food. Karyn, her mother, had prompted, "Don't forget the word prayer in prairie, Rachel." She'd put on record, which suited Harriet's Dante-like profile: Bette Davis in an original radio broadcast of *Jane Eyre*. Listening to one gravelly voice, she would hear the other, that touch of whiskey, that butterscotch burr of the hated tobacco. She leans forward. What is it they saw below the eyes of relentless brown? No matter what happens to burn my body, my spirit sees an eternal flame. As sun burned to crystal in the January seventh sky, Chel sat taking tea with Sarah Linen, who said, "I'm gathering up bits and pieces, took everything in for appraisal, rewrote the letter to my executor. That diamond-and-sapphire ring that my aunt bought before London: I could make a killing with it. And a killing is what I must make." Chel baked a batch of cranberry-nut bread; the tops were burned so she cut off the tops and torched the new tops with a little acetylene torch. Now they didn't look so naked. She hadn't done a lick of work baking. Janet had laid her collection of traveler's checks from one end to the other of the jeweler's black marble counter. I come from a long line of pawnbrokers," she'd winked, her eyes shining. She was another woman who'd sharpened her vision at the whetstone.

I go to sleep pondering whether to sell Maggie's old Singer sewing machine. Black with gold lettering, it's the very machine she sewed the star quilt with. Come hell or high water, I must hold on to it. Hell's bells. What spell's to be cast living so long?

Kay Kendrick had sailed away from heartbreak by divorcing her husband and buying a small sailboat. That, however, she swapped for the flute: sailing for song, the white gold that would never leave her. These were signature leave-takings: Kay Kendrick's after divorce. Now for Chel departure had come, like Jo's parting with convent life, like a crystal bowl that cracks and still leaves shards.

I see the fire of generations of jewelers, of sailors, burn down through mothers and daughters. "The Dutch kept furs and jewels," Janet had advised. No, I cannot shove away Maggith's Singer: that old black thing would bring no more than the cleaning woman's hill of tears.

Chapter Ten
When There's an Explosion, All the Birds Fly

Mark Twain said that the first week of a new year is the time to make
all those splendid resolutions. The second week you pave the road to hell
by violating them. I listen to Dvořák's *New World Symphony*, appropriate
for traveling from this world to the next.

Clay is the substance out of which things are made. Frame is the
boundary: limit, enclosure, containment. That night Chel decided
to take her grandmother Andréa's ancestral diamond to Sarah and to
Janet for appraisal. She had a lump in her throat twice as big as the
ring, which was large as a country church. She reminisced upon that
afternoon she and Dolly had ventured up in the attic to explore. The
two girls, with pipe-stem legs had discovered Mrs. Pearl Patch with her
one blind eye. Dolly had looked up at the dining ceiling and said, "Chel,
it's astronomy!" It was like the planetarium. In the gray-washed prairie
light, which earlier had been brazen, the little girls of seven were both
restless. They leafed through copies of the *Sears, Roebuck Catalogue*,
reading aloud to each other, they sensed the need for change. Seedlings
of light sprouted along with ice spines in the kitchen windows. There was
a cold wind. It was November. "Let's go explore the attic," I said to Dolly.
Let's!" she wiped crumbs off her lap, ever the more meticulous of us two.
Slowly, deliberately, we walked up each of the creaking attic stairs.

At the top stood Mrs. Pincushion beside Mrs. Pearl Patch, Mama's
dressmaking dummy. We looked up to see wheels of spiderwebs.
The light was the color of dark tea to our young eyes. I see it now as
parchment unrolling with a profound message to the world. There exists
no photograph. But picture two spindly-legged children in Nebraska
light in the early years of the twentieth century. Their pipe-stem legs,
however, have strong calves and drive them upstairs. I am afraid of my
own shadow these days. Back then we were intrepid. The space up the
stairs is vertical, cavernous. There is a buzz in the air; we were nervous
in a good way. I felt, since I preceded by one step literally that I led a
bravura performance. Eyes peered out at us from the top of the stairs:
they were bottoms. I put my arms around the mannequin I called Mrs.
Pearl Patch. "Let's dance," said the shyer Dolly, and we whirled and
whirled in a sort of preview of death one half year later, in the attic light
so brittle that if you took a match to it, it would be tinder. We decided to
try on floppy hats. There was an old blue boater and a green straw one. I
was born first, by two minutes; Dolly was the breach. Did this embolden
me for life? Our shared lives were short; my shadow self died Am I not

eternally seeking? Dolly stumbled, skinning her knee when she struggled
to reach a box on top of a trunk. I caught her; we both swayed, dizzy. I
saw cornflowers spin and spin. Wasn't it then that the burnt raspberry,
mulberry, and indigo colors of the star quilt began formulating in my
mind.

We sat on the wooden attic floor, having discovered a dusty ancient
mechanism of a merry-go-round. We began spinning and spinning it
until we were mesmerized, totally unhinged. Now cups and saucers
for doll tea parties were abandoned: we lost all sense of time until our
mother called upstairs in a loud but girlish soprano, "Dorothea, Rachel,
are you up there? If so, come clamber right down." We looked at each
other, eyes wide as saucers. Our first thought was to hide from Karyn's
voice; our second was to mobilize. Our nearly paralyzed feet shot out
from under us, and we thundered down the rickety wooden attic stairs,
leaving the wooden horses spinning behind us. "Dolly!" she caught my
twin in her arms, "Rachel!" she frowned. We were given no latchkey
to the attic door, so this was a forbidden thing. Obedient we were, but
always with mischief in our eyes. We knew there would be no corporal
punishment, but there might be a confiscated doll. We drew our breath
in till it stung our lungs. In those moments fleeing downstairs, I had
one of my mystic, out-of-the body experiences: I saw the mirrory ghost
of myself above the real girl fleeing in a cloud of pale chemicals, a
vision. When our father, the minister, came home and switched into
his Beethoven wing collar, we knew we would get added admonition.
Those gray eyes spoke as many volumes as an ink well, but they were
understated: words of elegant script on which parchment bond his eyes
would speak to us yet never utter a word. Dolly and I lay awake a long
time that night in our side-by-side bunk beds. Who knows who lay
awake longer, but I felt I had been exiled to Siberia and walked all night
on pipe-stem legs across the icy tundra of that remote northern land, a
preternatural version of our own. In my nightmare, six pallbearers bore
my doll-size body in satin. Tonight, wanting to take sacrament but not
communion, I tremble on that matchstick ladder staircase again.

*

Chel observes an iconic contrast between Jo and Harriet as she did
between Dolly and herself. Harriet had hands with liver splotches to
match her alcoholic complexion. Jo had Giacometti hands, talcum fine
with blue map veins standing out purply as rivers on antique vases.

Rachel dragged her feet home from Sarah Linen's house, where she
bartered her diamond in the outmoded setting, a collector's item, but
that's about it. Impoverished, odd, with her new paranoia, she swayed

back and forward on supple hips. As she slumped home through the icy village of Little Norway, she felt it akin to the Siberia she'd dreamed of at age seven alongside Dolly. Petrified, she almost felt that she had ceased to exist. She felt like a transient, an unwelcome vision. The place, their town was locked down by three p.m. All shades were halfway down. She was seeking asylum in a town that had become hostile to her. She felt like a character out of a Dostoevsky novel, maybe Prince Myshkin.

Secrecy is intolerable in love affairs. Jo's observation comes back to her as strange: you and I, she had said recently, are like those in London when the bombs stopped. Whenever men are blasting, with each dynamite ignition, the sky is filled with the black shapes of birds. Whenever there's an explosion all the bids fly. "I feel rootless," she had told Jo.

"Let's go home, Chel, and light a fire. It would be heaven to feel the heat on our back, my hips. Chel thought back on that dialogue, as she walked home to her room in this dream town.

At home she stares at the Norman Rockwell cutout of an old issue of *The Saturday Evening Post*. Two ordinary freckled boys, thoroughly hometown American, are on the cover. She brews tea. She knows those boys. One of her brothers? No, her brothers were stockier, not the reedy type. Birds nest in old rusted helmets.

Chel shut off the tea, lay down, put her palms on her eyes. Braille. She could read through her veins. After the explosion lit up the earth, would all fall back into utter blackness?

Josepha had a black convent mackintosh she still wore when it rained. Chel imagined she was putting a tracer upon all the lost letters back to their beginnings in this wilderness, this world. She knocked back three brandies and straight away opened the manuscript of Maggie's history of her life as a photographer. "It was part of my late-life experience to want to encounter the wilderness held within." Those alabaster dolls Dolly and she had seen on the fearful afternoon of their attic foray came back to Chel.

I encounter wilderness yearly, hourly. I recall first-day issues of stamps; holding them I felt an honor in what was an ordinary profession after all. When stamps of the Great Lakes appeared, I saw us on one: so blue, so legendary an image of our region. I feel special to none since Mother and Maggie are gone.

Chapter Eleven
Red Feather Duster

How tawny Maggith's gray-blonde hair had become. She wore a towel
and slacks. Naught on top. I didn't prolong the ritual. Cutting hair in
February leaves one cold, exposed. It is February once again. Last night
Jo asked me to cut her hair, and I thought of Maggie. Jo stood before
the smoky iron and handed me the scissors. She shook her hair out,
her collar bones thin, gleaming eggshell. Can one go no more into the
garden after sixty? I suddenly knew anguish. I wanted the possibilities
of Jo's life and of mine? To expand, tissue to stretch without rending.
It grew so dark before the hall mirror because the kerosene lantern
flickered out at Jo's. "We have to get away, Sister," I surprised myself
by whispering. "Away?" she asked. "From wartime London, must quit
romanticizing." "Chel, you are hungry at heart."

"Nobody would bite at the diamond ring." "To whom would you sell
your diamond ring? To Sarah, to Janet Clay. Ach, never mind! They are a
nest of strangers."

Maggie had said that she wanted to photograph an enemy bomb
straight out of the German furnaces, with its lethal curves, but no
one could get near them. Only captured enemy film exists. This was
how Rachel felt now. Jo put two thin hands on Rachel's shoulders to
steady her, then sat down on the kitchen chair. She said, "We are alive
at a moment of war, all of us, always." Chel is dizzy as Maggith chases
through snow with a red feather duster in hand. In the old primers girls
enact such activities: wood blocks show the child with a stout walking
leg, sturdy shoe laced. Maggie and Rachel in her own way each trembled
on against the tarnishing world. By late February Rachel no longer
resisted the impulse at midday to slip into the star quilt, wearing it as a
cape. She forced herself awake with a fifth cup of coffee. She signed Janet
Clay's book of callers in purple ink. Visitors had written here in a clear
curve, or large florid hand. Chel wrote in her post office hand.

*

If only the old cloth eight-pointed stars gave off any warmth or light.
"Are you making peace with the facts?" Jo asked hoarsely. "I am coming
to terms."

Rachel relived the day Maggie went off to photograph a steel plant.
It was like turning back a fingernail or peeling the flesh from a wound.
The welder's arc of flames was telling, scattering blue stars over her, their
oxyacetylene torches. Mag had watched numerous films on them and

came away unburned. Stirring a pea soup thick enough to stand a tin soldier in, Chel let the memory go.

I had had my fill but drove you with my attaché case, the one with the big baroque "R" on it. I drove you to the Greyhound station. You had an eight o'clock appointment with the foreman of the welding plant. I had dreamed of you in safety goggles, thick leather gloves, red fire extinguisher nearby. You borrowed my mountain boots so thick that your feet would not be cut by steel filings. I see the plant now rise up against winter night so often, you standing in the shower of sparks.

*

Sitting with Jo, the room stilled: the bonds between the two women were like joined wood. Rachel was fond of walking in the public park at nightfall. As a child she'd had a Roman Catholic friend, "Pity you're going to hell, Rachel, because you're so nice." She stiffened her backbone to no mail most evenings, but Burleson leaped up. Rachel found herself laughing out loud to the old dog. The telephone rang. It was Helga. "Rachel, I've some new puppets to bring over. Will you be in tonight?"

"Yes." Chel, brewing tea, saw the wooden faces with cheeks of flame and eyes of nut brown. Rachel soliloquized to the old sheepdog. The fault comes from this weakness in me, old girl, that now flows forth in age. No longer have I a buffer zone. The fault revolves around my having taken too much life from others, from girlhood on. The separation from Dolly. I cannot say where the full flaw comes from. If nobody visited, that would be the end of her voice for the night. She'd sleep early, Burleson at her feet, if she didn't read or work over her stamp collection. Perhaps, she though, I found too ripe a pleasure from Maggie.

The last time I kissed Margaret she wore her raffish brown velour hat, which I call her taxi hat. Maggie had nearly translucent eyes that could glow or change color like taffeta. They reflected how close to the end people were. Her camera perhaps brought safety the way one face will come up to another expecting a kiss but come up only against water or glass. The way you will pull on your old Irish sweater her eyes saw.

I woke to frost and sun. I must be getting somewhat crazed. I woke with the notion that I must slip away to a retreat, to that wooded monastery up north, with Jo. Are there Anglican nuns? Yes, she said, not just Catholic ones. Somewhere in my sleep last night the spiritual gambler broke even. I dreamed of a ship far at sea that resembles a turreted, bayoneted castle. Helga is coming over, but first a talky neighbor pops her head in the door. "I was in a funeral, Chel, when the snow started. Miserable weather," the neighbor shuddered. "Yes," Rachel said wearily, she'd been rewinding her braid. Had she the stamina of Sister Jo, who sat up nights two nights in a row with a fellow sister who was dying. Jo also sat with sick kids in the infirmary when she was principal. "I'm in awe of you," Chel said to Maggie in her gruff voice when she'd seen Maggie's early photos at the Y. "But I'll get over you."

Chapter Twelve
Runners and Nuns

Long-distance runner, the heart beats iron. During war, the Minister of Agriculture in England advised folk to dig for victory. Folk thought in terms of rotating crops as well as of color schemes. Rachel now thought of these schemes, which filled her with a terrible sense of hope. Was her personal war ending? Helga was coming. When spring is on the doorstep, Jo and she get nervous and argue over this, that. They went through the Depression together. "I saw my mother start patching seats and elbows more and more," Jo said. When spring was on the doorstep, why they become such wanderers? Why does Chel flash back to this time before Maggie dawned on her world? To shear away pain as though she were shearing a sheep. What you lose on the swings you make up on the merry-go-round. The cold becomes paralyzing; clothes are a weight that makes people move slowly. Humped in ice, the roads where Chel was a postal carrier, she can still remember feeling with her feet. I would run up and down stairs to stoops to keep warm. Maggie takes me in her arms, her teeth chatter, she rocks me on her breast as though I were an ancient child, "You a-a-a-re cold, you are fro-o-o-z-en, my poor mailman." In the star quilt, I recall the dream of my fiftieth birthday. It was a mask occasion. We were to move from one small shore house to another. Maggith, you were waiting for me. There was lots of wood around. Harriet came with Jo. The odd planes of Harriet's face, her height, her flat chest impressed me. There was Jo's nearly transparent gaze. She was holding one of the pipes I'd smoked, a small Swedish one. "Here, Chel, pewter candlesticks paintings. No, a print of a Rembrandt sketch. I lost my breath and walked on, bearing these two momentous gifts, the pewter and the Rembrandt. Was it a procession in a dream? I saw you, Maggie, in your smock blouse and gray slacks. Then you were lost to me. I called, "Margaret," my tone becoming urgent.

Reared on fairy tales, dream could be dangerously taken for fact. The community acted on promises as if they were facts. Chel tore the blue quilt off her and folded it at the foot of the bed trying to stave off grief. But not so. She closed her eyes seeing their smaller pieced quilt: double wedding ring, Amish, 1910–1929, Ohio. Rachel thought of the Dukabor community in Minnesota: red brick houses in the center; to right and left like hefty wings, grim and tight, where the married couples live on one side, the bachelors on the other. In the center house live the deacon and deaconess, virgins were kept away from the hands of fornicators.

Naught on earth sparkles with color.

*

One day out of the blue, Maggith took a curling iron to her hair. Her hair turned out like boiled milk. Chel loved it silky.

Listening to the train hoot on Store Street close to Regional Iron, Chel looked so cold she thought only of a hot tub. Jo's frailty had impressed itself upon Chel the way an engraved mark does on a coin. Bernhardt herself had spare eating habits. Sarah Bernhardt was like Maggie, who would fill the plate of photography with riches and satisfy herself with a white cream pitcher on a grainy Minnesota day. Helga just phoned, "I have the true clue to the puppets: they are puppets no longer. They have broken loose." Helga, I, too, am breaking free. What else do we endeavor but to become human puppets all our lives. Not a bit of it. I am walking along with Maggie tethered by exceptional cold one November morning. How have a high school art teacher and a postal worker struck such communion of color? Full-throated. Certainly Pitou and Bernhardt were a strange pair. At the end, the great director and great actress are alone, mutually hostile, which gives rise to volatile scenes. A book is thrown across a room, a costume, a shoe.

We worked on quietness, tooling. We were not Pitou and Bernhardt. Two old weathered lesbians we were who had been through much and wanted to come out without a streak of cruelty. But clearly we were cruel toward the end. "She is your Boswell, you her Johnson. It is simple as that," mother Karyn once told me. We are now down to three hours daylight, if that: eleven in the morning to two in afternoon, the time when the ice mist burns off and before the ducks descend. Well, as I draw the wings of this gray sweater about my ears, I am watching you, Mag, walking along the dark shore in Minnesota. Yoga straightens and directs your spine, which nonetheless may sway and bend like a willow. We have arrived at late January. I think of Hans Christian Andersen, melting a hole with a penny in a windowpane. I sold Mother's diamond for two hundred, got the car out of the shop, battling the weight and trials of the body and my clothing. You have found a pebble and skip it along water. Burleson chases a ball of white dancing fire. You wear green windbreaker, collar, and an extra pair of ears. I don't know why I go on baking you apples when you're careless as the ship boy and leave them in the pan only to blacken. Striding with an anger that animates, an anger that give you wings on your heels like Hermes the messenger. Or now you wear a sweater and brown suede jacket with mock fur since you don't wear dead animals. You bought it at Second Snowfall, the shop next to Sweet Cherubim, where you bought us a gift of apple cheesecake. Two old cherubim, we scoff it. You, old thing, I say to myself, staving off darkness at heart, one step ahead of melancholy, taking in the lens the dark curving scimitar shore of wintertime, the battlement of buildings as in dementia leaning back under a lidded silver sky. There was always another day and another day until there were no more. Bernhardt at the end was seventy-nine, and Pitou saw the fleshly frame sheared away. One leg left, one had been amputated, one lung, too, was gone. Only ardor remaining.

The oddly shaped Great Lakes are inland oceans. They could be the vast blue hoof prints left by Babe the Blue Ox. I see brick circular chimneys lowered by chains, down through clouds, for Babe and Paul to pass. Then I look down to you, almost unfinished: crystallized amid all that greenery or snow white. You would narrate with a severe tinge. "Chel, we've only begun to scratch the surface in photography: frame, resolution, focus. There's a new heroism at hand. Pockets for stashing film, nails to photograph, a clutch of anything, the riches of earth. You liked to shine up nails with oil then place them on a black bench or sill. I could reach in my hand and pull out a tube of sap green, hip pockets, breast pockets to feel you under. "You sly fox," you'd say. Desire is not dead in the old. To me kids used to bring their sick birds. Nightingale Chel, I was given to nursing foxes, cats, when I was nine or ten. One way or other I'd rig up a splint for a hurt wing, but I cannot fix us now, sweet thing.

Chapter Thirteen
A Whole New Set of Listeners

Maggie went off to teach high school students art in thick wool stockings and no-nonsense shoes. In Maggie's year of absence a whole new set of listeners had evolved from waiting in the wings. Did they whisper that she was unfair to Mag? That she as the older woman had lorded it over her sweetheart? She could ride the horse of grief now with unrelenting stride, but she would ride ill will. Her honor was her badge. Helga brought over her largest puppet and ran through a speech like running a red hot poker or a needle through Chel's heart. When Helga bowed the head of the puppet in a curtain line, Chel read the gesture as sacrificial. She memorized the expression in those carved features, lips, and hands on Helga's jeans, chips of clay. They were not marionettes but large wood heads with thin hands. Helga's human mind, would they meet somewhere in ice fields?

Chel recalled Old Miss Petticoat. Old Miss Petticoat was the stiffest thing alive, and she loathed kids. She was children's librarian in Little Norway. "Please ma'am, can you suggest a good book for an inquisitive girl of seven?"

"An inquisitive girl of seven need not ask." Her white scalloped petticoat always hung down in back. She must have lived with mother or maiden aunt. We stuck out our tongues. After Helga left, Chel crawled under the covers without eating. Maggie had laughed. Closing her face to the dark, she saw the puppeteer coming down the street again the next day. Who else had a caller who came with wood head in both arms and lips waiting to be kissed? Rachel drew back the curtain past midnight. Only one person on the street, thin, ghastly, her chest caved in it was "the woman who talked to her cigarette." They knew no other name. She lived alone. She held her cigarette about a foot from her mouth as you passed her, spoke to it, her small companion. "Well, little friend, how are you keeping?"

Sleep, Chel. Don't lug the sorrows of the past on your back. "I protected her fiercely," the first voice came. "Nonsense. That's the way of love." The five and twenty soldiers were made from one spoon. When they got to the last one, there was only enough tin for one leg. He was mostly filled with valor. He burned for the love of the paper ballerina. Chel slipped out of bed, the star quilt cape around her back.

The tin soldier stood there lighted up by flame. He looked at the dancer. He felt that he was melting, but he stood firm, shouldering his gun. Then suddenly the door opened, a draft of air caught the dancer. The fairy tale ended with the ballerina flying straight into the fire. She blazed and was gone.

*

She slammed the book. Her brain was on fire. Margaret has her genius. Could I have mine? I will ride the horse slowly through the wild wood of the world. She had to clear her honor. She would put Maggie's prints in order in her own collection. Slowly she saw the silvers of the scene assemble themselves. What if Maggie's clothes caught fire in the night? Helga bowed the puppet's huge wooden head and made unkissable lips speak. Helga conveyed with the hands a passion that was human.

PART TWO

Chapter Fourteen
In the Cabin (Under Silver and Low Sky)

They said a woman couldn't endure here. I lie on my back in this log cabin. A spot of rust moves, red quilted flame, halts on snow. It breathes. It is a bird. I am wearing one quilt over two sweaters and a down jacket. I sit on a low bed, a pallet covered by one of the lowest-toned quilts I made. It's a one-room log cabin I've rented until spring. Looks like a weave, or wave of snow out the window. I'll endure. I've lost one or two battles but will win the war.

It feels like I'm eight months with child. I can close my eyes and change this snow to rain. It is Easter morning when I dash out to shoot the rain rabbit. He has eyes of rain, fur of rain, paws of rain. He carries baskets of rain eggs. I come back dripping into the house to Chel. I stand in yellow oilskin and black Wellingtons in a shining puddle. This reminds me of our trip down the Thames. It rained all the time. Chel kept catching me from falling backward. I wore my brim hat to avoid sun wheels. It was my chance of a lifetime. What could Chel expect? Christ! I had so little time to get all this carved upon silver plate with less than a gram of sodium. She kept saying I was bound and determined to fall ass over teakettle into the polluted Thames.

"Where will you be then, my girl, one eye, maybe even two, clogged with the Thames?" This was a example was of Chel's controlling ways. I never did fall backward, however. Instead, she yanked me forward every time. Domineering beloved. We learned more from our tour guide than we ever wanted to learn. We'd rather have hoofed it alone through London and environs, but the church tour was within our budget, damn their holiness and pious platitudes! All those churches and cathedrals the guides pointed out. I could have done with more byways of London, although I shot all I could possibly photograph of the gold of Christopher Wren St. Paul's. If I'd only been able to shoot St. Paul's during the bombings. I was overflowing with unfulfilled longing that whole time in London. We took the inland waterways, toured the Old Bulldog's Secret World War II command post in London which is subterranean and next to the Thames. I longed to do a series of stills but was forbidden. Shoreline battles were fought there during the seventeenth century. Chel and I fought our own. It seemed she was intent upon laying the blueprint for my future then. "Why do I get the sense you'd rather be with some one else?" I can recall saying in a small London teashop with diamond-leaded glass panes.

"With whom?" she asked her husky voice breaking.

I shrugged. She was the one who bellowed after me when I ran out the door to photograph "Wear Biscuit, wear Toast!" I turned "Maggie, wear Parchment." So it was that she would clothe me by daily selecting my shirts, but I streaked out my own way with a red feather duster in the sun.

I loved London. I grew impatient for more. The cheeky sparrows, the cheeky people. I surprised myself one day by declaring that I was a Limey at heart. We were always on the dash in those days, a tongue of scarf sticking out of a valise. Our years together were like the rings of a tree or the rings around Saturn. They revolve now slowly in me. Christmas, New Year's, birthdays. This Yule I yearned to hear Chel's voice but not the breakdown. I wanted to say Happy Yule, but I was the one who had done the leaving after all.

The sky now was an oyster quilt with a crimson sun shining from it. Now it was ominous pewter. Maggie had a one-year lease on the cabin, which was only forty miles above the town where she taught a twice-weekly one grad course in black-and-white photography. Here was far enough from civilization that what was wild in her could be stilled against a scarcely moving background. England, it rang such bells. I felt that when we got away five years ago, we were in a strange space. A sympathy seemed lost between Chel and me. She could not see that I wanted to scrape all our funds together and stay. "There's Scarstown, Harrowgate, Maggie. There's Battlement Square back home. There's Turret Street with all its antique shops. You've hardly begun to shoot them."

"Ach, Chel, I've had those all my life. I love those streets, but I've plumbed them" No, she didn't see. Old English faces in the bed-and-breakfast places, even my harrowing driving on the wrong side of the road that I promised to master if we could only stay. It was a source of bitterness that she could not see my love affair with London. For courtship purposes, we put our best foot forward. We were no longer in our heyday, and I was courting London. Luck had it that they were almost able to rent a loft in London with northern light, something Maggie had wanted all her life. There had been pure halcyon days in England, when the air was narrative, a watercolor itself. Chel was contented to mosey in her large floppy hat, "There is something sweet and sensible about you, Maggie," she said "especially in England."

Am I going back one hundred years to being a pioneer woman? In England I bought Chel a small set of watercolor circles she could slip into her purse or her London Fog raincoat, a block of watercolor paper, and some small brushes. England might bring out her artistic streak, but I caught her sketching only once.

*

Maggie wore leather boots. She wore a long skirt; a small stream ran by the cabin. She washed her cropped gray-blonde hair in the stream; she also washed laundry there in fine weather. Since October it had been frozen solid. What things of civilization were present? Annie Dillard's *Pilgrim at Tinker Creek*, the King James Bible, the collected poems of Elizabeth Bishop. Of Dillard she'd brought the paperback edition, more pages dog-eared than not. This was her go at life in the wilderness. She had a framed black-and-white portrait of Chel. Hers, Maggie mused, is a face that has become less, not more, readable with time. I have been so richly companioned by this face, which has weathered well. I see us as two old fighters in the ring. Rachel's gait and voice ruled. It was her size. Some change in me prompted troubles amid the sweetness that always returned for a day or a week. Yes, I felt a change in me as real as a child forming, or a ton of coal, a shock of wheat, a gram of sodium, with their various and predictable effects. I'd urged Chel to build the greenhouse wing. I footed the bill, but it turned out to be only two years before my departure. All glass and light, it was a photographer's dream.

*

Meaning floods like sun, like shooting stars. I do not make excursions into physics; it is when I am a bit gone that I speculate on the wheels in the sun. On summer nights Chel and I would drive to the local vegetable farm. We'd buy spinach, beets, lettuce, apples. People would come out irate despite the lushness of the produce. "I don't know how they can call these strawberries. Did you see the insides of those mushrooms?" The wrath of society, the steam and vapor of civilization clouded the day and then sank. She did not miss drinking highballs with Harriet, who was as elegant as a harlequin. It turns blue, the sky behind Little Norway Town Hall in November. I miss that. Leaves are all swept then. We traveled through England arm in arm, like figures cut from an old daguerreotype of two Boston blue stockings. What are the things I miss of civilization? The ritual of mornings; Townson, our cat; and Burleson, our dog. England. I didn't want our love to change. There was something daring, handsome in my new freedom but the strangeness of sleeping in separate rooms? Did most of our friends look upon my departure as my taking leave of my senses? What England did besides crystallize a conflict beneath the surface was to show me how a world can rise from ashes: gutted buildings, bombed-out churches and cathedrals. I felt and seized the power for change and regeneration in myself. A long rail journey would have been exhilarating, spending hours with someone like Helga or Nellie could have been full. But those were not the main things I wanted. I needed what a serious child requires: uninterrupted dream time. Retirement threw us into such closeness that time was eclipsed, ironically, by closeness which forbade sharing. One must always have some of oneself to oneself. One cannot share all things. Finally I was able to share nothing. But a leave-taking is a leave-taking, and it is shocking.

Uncouth have I become? All the things Chel loved me for when we were young, all those traits that made me grab the bull by the horns and have my photographs included in the exhibit of women photographers, were those leaving me? I had the body to move and the mind to make me obey. I ask, am I still Maggie? Am I living fully now or merely surviving? Cheerful and hardy—those are good things. Sullen and wasted—those traits I shun. Will Chel and I last through the winter into spring?

"So you think me daft to want the loft in London?"

"We've only let Widdershins for half a year. I think we've sunk a small fortune into the greenhouse.

"Ach, the greenhouse." The loft faced north. I wanted to put together an exhibit that would recoup our loss. I thought my way back to the airline pilot, his loft in the beige house, himself sailing over green grass, blue prairie into a night of stars. Antoine de Saint-Exupéry. It is for love we do what we do, for an odd, battered type love I did this thing. From the aerie of my loft I could have watched storms roll over London.

Maggie socialized with young students in town; she magnetized some but rarely brought one up to the cabin. Listening to music reminded her of Chel. She didn't listen often. In summer she'd gone fishing for brook trout, fried the tasty fish to a crackle over a fire by the water. She'd boned up on running, caught up on some of the athletic skills she abandoned in her forties. She had a bottle of brandy and had built a rich inner life in autumn and winter evenings. She smoked heavily all the time, a cigarette hanging from her lower lip. Maggie cultivated a postage-stamp garden in summer, chopped wood in autumn, banked fires and read late into winter nights, sometimes until three a.m. I'm catching up, she thought. But there was something else that was happening; it was as if the very cells in her brain and body were being slowly, painfully replaced by other cells, like cells of porous light in stone changing through the centuries, or molecules altering that create the colors in a painting. What the human community thought of her back home mattered. In this she was like Rachel, who feared being ostracized. They might gradually come to understand her choice, or they might never understand. Solitude has watered my love, not my doubts, and my love has grown greener.

Maggie battled. She dreamed. This was no greater wilderness than home was, simply a different kind. Did it have to do with frontiers, with

finding a new boundary to the self? Something in one pushes its way out.
I always felt the novice with Chel despite my strength in photography,
despite the way I could speak through light. I felt tongue-tied, my hands
tied. When I could speak more strongly through photography than
in words, that became a wild and desperate voice in me that wanted
freedom and an art I wanted to rest, to wrest, from.

I wanted to rest from the invading angel for a year. Chel assumed I
wanted more time to create. I see a world as clearly blue as a Dresden
lake. But a bomb struck, and domestic war shattered the country I
extolled. Marital peace had become for me the landscape of the twenty-
third Psalm. If Chel were here with me, we'd talk all night. We'd take
the VW with its snow tires and chains down into town and whack snow
off the mailbox. She'd chew me out for driving this Bug around. She'd
badger me, saying that if I had any practical sense I'd have bought myself
a four-wheel-drive pickup to camp in the woods for a year. But then there
was little time to talk.

Sister Jo was a woman apart, a winter bird with a circle of questions
rimming her daily. Questioning faith became her daily devotional.

My albums of shots, many of my contact sheets are back home. In
one way, I see myself as a pioneer woman at the edge of a breakthrough.
In another way, I am a woman running away, a burned child. Burned
children are always problem children. The black apron of night I see
as an apron stage reaching into an invisible audience. Then no seen
audience, only the felt one. Chel and I turned slowly as the peacock does
from the sun. The big changes in life are made by a slight turning of the
earth under our feet.

How I have darkened Chel's life I cannot tell. I hope she is better off
than I am. Solomon, when asked what one gift he most wanted, asked
for the gift of understanding.

Maggie had a sudden craving for Chinese food. A loss of community
struck her. The snowflakes were dense out her window in late day: a
white-silver weave against a pewter sky occurred. No more Delft plate.
She has an image of Chel, dreaming and cursing her way through a
long evening of arranging stamps. Maggie had met Laura Gilpin in New
Mexico at a convention of women artists. She had considered spending
this year in New Mexico photographing adobes homes of rosy brown
and the winding red roads of Santa Fe. Chel loved the desert, where
they once spent a summer, but the northern woods had an even stronger
claim on Maggie. How odd tonight to come across in the pages of a book
Renoir's painting "Luncheon of the Boating Party," which depicted
happy young men and brawny women, with shirtsleeves rolled up in
some boathouse on the banks of the river, drinking, throwing back their

heads and laughing. Yet there was something strangely dislocated about
them. She felt she had come upon some misplaced French gaiety. In
contrast, Maggith was stormed by images of Sister Jo still in the convent,
head bent, hands clenched, privately arguing with God.

My marriage with Chel I can see as a cathedral sunk into the sea.
The sunken cathedral. In another way we are still moving through those
rooms of Widdershins but more slowly, our limbs slowed by water, our
speech and breathing measured more slowly too. Sweetbreads. Chel
would cook them and we'd laugh, what foods these morsels be. I see
our partnership as a great ship glowing in the night, a ghost ship. I hear
Chel's isolated phrase, "Press on," and wonder about human tenderness,
for I did and do feel tender toward her. We play chess, the game of kings,
a game of war. In lightning moves Chel proceeds. I wonder if women's
women are always isolated and love to cook. Chel does not care for
this subject. I wear "Sky," the blue nightgown. I think she feels like a
mother toward me. Our marriage is a skiff, moving across the night like
a slow ruler across the margin of the ocean, crossing the Bering Strait of
imagination.

"One more year in London?"

"A nurse studies discipline. A photographer studies discipline. A lover
knows the lifelong habit of discipline. No, Margaret, I tell you no for a
final time."

*

You are inured to the postman's creed of delivery come hail, sleet,
snow, or rain. I am snowballing. I am rolling downhill gathering speed
like a snowball. I will crash soon, and I keep contemplating the strength
of women. By the way a lover lights his lady's cigarette under a lamppost
in a 1940s movie, you know theirs is an illicit affair. That way you know
a thing is coming to an end. "Here, beloved," you say in one of your rare
tender moments, "I have healing in my hands. You have in yours too. Put
them on the back of my neck. I placed my sinewy hands on the dowager's
hump, which is increasing, and can imagine the pain of this deformity at
the top of the spine.

Rachel. I see the mail sack. I smell the glue of the mailroom she
worked in all those years. The few fine photographs I was able to draw
up from the darkness now swim before my eyes. Goodnight, cabin,
Goodnight, snow. Goodnight, Townson, whom I have taken, and
Burleson, whom I have left at home. Now the house is all quiet, black,
inside itself except for Burleson's batting a rabbit in her dream. Time in
the darkroom moved as in a dream. I'd catch Rachel in the door at times,
arms akimbo, smiling. Then she'd turn back to her baking. I am teaching

the eight-year-old son of a friend cross-country skiing. I love the feel of
a child's hand in mine. Stirring up oatmeal the color of her sweater,
standing over the cook stove, conjuring fifteen profiles of women, her last
exhibit.

Back to Christmas when I was eight years old. Mama had given me
the Brownie camera. I'd slip off to the woods with it. When Mama died
of double pneumonia, my three brothers were farmed out to one aunt,
and I got tall and lavender Aunt Cornelia, who already had four children
of her own, no girls, only boys. The little box became my friend. "You
are my soul, not just my eyes." I kept it by my pillow on the tall, rickety
night table. I could hear feathers in my pillow chatting to one another.
"You are too imaginative," Aunt Cornelia warned. She told me that I,
Maggie, was average in all ways except one: daydreaming. When I turned
fourteen, I'd saved up enough to trade in the old Brownie. I saw fresh
woods, a new earth and sky.

I read Blake because my cousin Brigitta, who was two years younger,
was given an illustrated copy of Blake's *Songs of Innocence and of Experience*.
I coveted one of my own, and Aunt Cornelia rapped me on the knuckles
telling me, "You have a tendency to covet things." "Only wondrous
things," I countered. I try to feel a mother's touch again but see father,
toolmaker. When I visited him and the boys in summer, Father showed
me handmade nails, glistening in their oils, hammers, tongs. "Look,
Maggie, how the small wood horses are turning on the miniature merry-
go-round."

"Papa! You've made it for me." He had. It was my fourteenth
birthday. He has used his spare hours to carve little horses of white
pine, their dowels perfectly joined so that not a nail could be seen. In
the rough-hewn worlds of the north among icebergs and forests, he
lived in my imagination. "Papa, the horses turn silently," "They make
music if you listen." Those horses inspired my collection of prints for
northern Minnesota's toy museum at their centennial. I shot twenty-five
photographs of antique toys.

I have spent enough time alone with Chel, Maggie decided, impatient
with her clothing, tearing off the quilted vest.

*

She had two large wooden boxes of notes on a lifetime in
photography. She'd transferred them from banker's boxes. Sixty-four
years of age, many of embattled living. "Countess Impatience," Rachel
would say. Kneeling to take up Townson's dish of milk, Townson who
went "ron, ron, ron," Maggie felt a sharp twinge in her back across the
back of her lungs. She thought of Brigitta as she straightened. Brigitta

was the thin one in the family, thin and sensitive, with flaxen hair and bangs, the kind of hair people imagine children of Norwegian descent have. Brigitta was a godchild who Cornelia had taken under her wing and regarded as a daughter. She was the ideal daughter, the tall, golden-haired one. Maggie was the upstart. What am I doing this year alone that I could not have done with Rachel? Finished growing up perhaps, roughed it. In early spring there were trees budding and limitless camera light. How strange it was to have no one to return to in the evening. It drains warmth from my work. But why am I surprised? I seem to have chosen a different vision, maybe a starker one. Yet ever since I was a girl, I've loved stark things. Even the toys I photographed, boats and dolls, were stark. A white plate on a kitchen table drew me.

When we had shaken the last coin out of the piggy bank, there was little left. I went to my favorite shop, the typewriter shop in Little Norway. Old Underwoods and the light around people. When you love someone, there is a light around them.

Maggie set the pen down. Living so far up the canyon, she could not catch the sound of the midnight train, the mark that split night from morning in Little Norway. Often she observed masses of people at railway stations. She shot Jo with the light around her, which made her look like a spiky Byzantine saint, with rolling pin in hand, a stark angel in the kitchen. We each battled our angel. After many years I abandoned my stone angels that pouted. Spoiled babies, they were the seraphim and cherubim of my childhood. Chel was a riled stone angel of a woman those last years. I had the lance of the camera and tripod in hand.

"I like your name. It is so solid; it has a ring, like Matthew," Jo said. I like Chel's name. It goes with her sensual voice. I lie awake thinking of the voice capable of projecting to others, deep-barreled. Often ample-breasted women are as throaty as wood pigeons. Chel was older when we met, more grown up, whereas I was drawn, almost torn, in two directions, my child, my woman, as though I were pulled by horses, quartering me limb from limb. You are headlong, Maggie," she said. "I'm a bull, Taurus." Disenchanted, she wanted me to remain gallant, gamine. I packed all Rachel's letters in boxes and took them with me. Tied powerfully, all in the bold cursive learned in elementary schoolroom. These letters spoke of the most everyday things. From time to time, shifts would occur, and shafts of light would be thrown as she delved into philosophy and religion. Rachel wrote of transitions as she spoke of changes when we were in conversation. We'd be talking easily at one level through evening, then all at once we would shift to a level we hardly knew existed, cutting through doubt. It was as if the sun had come out, a silver Arctic disc in our hand at midnight. Conversation. "You crave a struggle to break free of the enclosures of your life now that we have the greenhouse, Maggie." The wind cuts like a lion's tooth. "I have mellowed, Margaret," Chel softened her tone. "You may find a pleasant change. I think I am becoming as reclusive as a Trappist monk."

Chapter Fifteen
Our Towhee

Chel hoarded every scrap of suet, bacon rind, and meat for the
towhees, which Maggie followed with monk-like attention. Maggie let
her eye unroll on Rochester, New York, Kodak town. Visiting the George
Eastman House with Chel in the days of basic black, pearls, and bobbed
hair. Maggie had mixed feelings about like the dreamy gelatins of Eugène
Atget's sepias. He was called the photographer of the century. Most
of all, Maggie was drawn by the albumens of Julia Margaret Cameron.
Looked at from one perspective, these were ethereal women, but seen
from another, their square jaws and strong hands made them seem as
tough as the fellows in the mines. These were faces straight out of Willa
Cather's Nebraska; these were women from Red Cloud who had crossed
the plains.

Eye is the same spelled backward as forward. Chel used to say I lived
with my eye focused, that my eye framed life. "And you," I would counter,
"observe postage stamps, marks, everything transmitted as messaged
invisible to your own eye." What an ironic pair, as Rachel positively
ached to see, uncover, and understand the unseen messages.

Glass jars. When the medical school said that I could come and
photograph embryos in formaldehyde, it was an eye-opening experience
of a lifetime. There the eye of the child was in the womb in the ancient-
appearing huge head. There the body floated effortlessly. I did my series
of ten embryos at different stages of pre-birth. Last night I saw a collage
of postage stamps in a dream. I rinsed the acrylics off my palette, and
Chel stood in the door. It was a dream but it would have been splendid.

There was my palette, set in the dish drain, all colors wet as though
they had been oiled: hooker's green, burnt sienna, raven black. I was a
girl of slender means to whom Chel turned once in Kew gardens and
said, "Margaret, I think you have a typically English face."

"What's that?"

"Determined, clear-cut profile." I got the message and thought of
"Come down to Kew in lilac time (it isn't far from London!)."

Flying to my various shows in midlife, I soared above the brown-and-
white frozen patchwork of winter. I imagined I saw the train, that dot
of iron bearing Chel in it slowly toward my exhibitions, for as sure as
the lord made little green apples, she would not fly. I'd fly, she'd train.
I'd meet her at the railway station, feel her large, leather-gloved hand
in mine. I can still see the ancient, huge camera on the marble ground
floor of the Eastman mansion. I saw the first color prints, delicate, hand-

touched. I kept holding hard, however, to my belief that the thorny heart of love was most workable in black and white. Ansel Adams shot nature, which few women photographers have been interested in. Dorothea Lange photographed people. Steichen, on the other hand, photographed "New York in Snowstorm." He'd sat for hours to capture that dreamy wash of whites. Walker Evans caught families with angry expressions after a long journey. He conveyed the truth that life is a long, difficult journey.

Rachel sent me a carton of cigarettes! In this morning's mail she had written back to me about the quote by E. M. Forster I mailed last week: "What he says about love, Maggie, is tough-minded, generous, even humorous. What he said was that 'people must go away from each other (spiritually) every now and then and improve themselves if the relationship is to develop or even endure.'" Chel has the tact not to touch down too hard on this question. She wrote, "I like his comment. We are more complicated, however, Maggie, and also richer than we know. Affection grows more difficult than it was in youth but, with luck, also more glorious."

Maggie set the carton of opened cigarettes by the bed. She folded the letter four times. Jo had never spiritually left the convent. At times was theirs a marriage à trois? It had a triangular quality, so that when she'd seen Chel's head bobbing in the car with Harriet's frizzy aureole, it got her Irish up. Harriet's union with Chel was a strange, indefinable union. No, it was not a marriage of three. Forster's quote began "Personal relationships seem to me to be the most real things on the surface of the earth" Did Chel's writing and mailing the forbidden cigarettes affirm Maggie's desires? Did this act say, look, I understand that we must go away from each other in order to return?

How can I write back that I miss the jumble of overdue library books lying on our table? Life went to hell in a handbasket many days, Maggie thought, striking a match, opening the first of the neat cellophane packs of cigarettes, but why did I make such a ruckus over staying in London? Was I behaving like a spoiled child?

I miss the ring of the telephone, even the damned phone.

Maggie rubbed the scruff of her neck, rose recklessly, then strode out the door, smoking with her head bent. Today no profile was visible of those hills that made up the old woman of the mountain. With a bold stride, she advanced, recalling traveling from Milwaukee back to Little Norway clutching her Sunday *St. Louis Post-Dispatch*. Rerouted because of blizzards in the Midwest, she'd carried it through three airports. Rachel always had her radar screen, that delicate dish atop the human mountain, tuned to Maggie's signs of exhaustion, the exhaustion that came after raiding the fridge for Swedish rye, cheese, black-forest ham. Chel would take a hard look at Mag, as though for the first time. "You've used your lot of energy. You've about done yourself in." Declaring this, Chel would turn back the star quilt and thump pillows.

I am here, thought Maggie, in this cabin, neither desperate nor satisfied living out my year, restless to be preparing with Chel a decadent dinner of scalloped potatoes, stuffed cabbage, sausages in barbecue sauce.

Covent Garden. The Convent. Yes, Maggie had seen Chel lean over and give Jo in her black convent mackintosh that long kiss in the car's front seat, then come into those eyes moist, throat husky. Maggie had known to let well enough alone. This low storm sky reminded Mag of those days at the Eastman Rochester Museum, days that were submerged in a certain dark reality. They'd visited before the first snows tipped that industrial city, that brick and mill and water town. Chel used to curse me like an old sea salt for smoking, but she was the one with a voice as hoarse as an ancient sailor. Snow was now thickening in the cabin window.

Maggie thought about the way the lime in Rachel's gin would collect bubbles. She photographed the ice cubes in a gin and tonic. Maggie used to perk up every time there was a hearse for sale. She loved the old roadsters. She wanted one for Rachel.

The snow stopped. Individual icicles shone like a crystal beard along the roof. On such days when Chel was young, she would announce, "Mailwoman!" and throw back her head laughing. Recalling this image of her even with a shopping list as long as my arm in one pocket and the house key in the other, we could not have been married too long. On freezing winter mornings, I'd see our hot-water bottle in its cover made to resemble a lamb with a black satin tail. Who wanted to empty it? It became so heavy in the morning. Rachel, I hear you when you talk about our community. Maggie unfolded the letter. "The fabric of the community isn't the same without you, Mag. Jeb and Anna are having a hard go since Jeb fell. She said he makes it hard for her to get any sleep, up and down like a yo-yo. I asked if he gets lonely when she goes out shopping, but Anna says Jeb is so far gone he doesn't know what lonely means. She says she'll hold on as long as she can."

Jedidah. He'd changed the name to Jeb as a boy. Going through her own changes, Mag began reviewing the changes great photographers had gone through: Ansel Adams began life as a musician, a pianist and organist. Eugène Atget was an actor until he turned to photography at forty-one. Wynn Bullock was another musician, who used his voice and words until yet another seed took root that made him distrust words. She thumped snow off her boots after testing the air this morning. Atget, like me, saw photography as a cross between economy and art. He ate only bread, sugar, and water. His life was devoted to frugality. She saw the series he had done of children, kids with ancient, frightened expressions. Harriet's baby photo was arresting: she had fierce black eyes, as sharp as an insect's, a thin face, and an aureole of curls. Harriet's face was disturbing even then.

Doorways. Atget loved doing doorways. Maggie preferred doorways with people in them. They knew mainly couples of women, but there were Jeb and Anna, one of about four man-and-woman couples whose histories were woven into Chel and Maggie's life as warp and woof. Then there was Zilpha and Fred, another solid pair of farming folk who were yoked by labor.

Staircases had captured Maggie's eye at one point. Nothing, however, riveted her continuously so much as the human face: a couple in a domestic scene reflected the movement of hidden needs as a mirror might. These mornings when she could see every twig outlined in ice did not challenge the way a face or a foot on a stair does. She tossed her red wool stockings from England into the corner by the fire. Only in England could she buy such wool. Keating Road, Charing Cross. That moment when folk exchanged worried glances was another she sought to capture. The challenge was capturing the calm of couples that were so damned handsome as Zilpha and Fred, Jeb and Anna.

The whole world is my favorite subject. I sought to learn drawing, but the teachers made drawing dull; they inevitably began with an apple, a pear, then a table, a sailboat on a lake for perspective, far and near. The male and female form came next. It was rigid.

There seemed no sane solution to our money problems. There seemed no politic move but to rush out the door of our flat those numerous morning in London when you, Chel, slept off a hangover until noon. I managed, also slightly hungover, to slip out by sheer dint of will at seven to catch early light that englobed the city, wrapping St. Paul's dome in gold, like a freshly hatched egg. For me it was a wondrous yet terrifying time. We were on thin ice. European hostels have double beds. Pale and virginal like saints laid in tombs, we each held fast to our wood bedstead. Cloth stars could warm, and wood could enclose when we were together.

"For me, the camera is a sketchbook," writes Henri Cartier-Bresson. That summer in England Chel's eyes looked faded, the pupils a duller shade. Banisters in England had fascinated me. The Victorian homes were like some back in Little Norway, but I, too, ran out of energy. There were solid brass knockers on doors in Tudor homes. I wanted to examine, reveal, shatter the genteel world, myself an iconoclast. But how could I? There were winters when I felt that the Little Ice Age was returning. I pictured the world shrouded, encased: homes in bubbles, igloos. The public library, the bank, the post office. We watched birds in our backyard, Widdershins from the kitchen window. There weren't many birds that winter. I tried to photograph the towhee, but the terms were harsh: my speed had to be great. Chel, too, was enthralled by the miniature shiny head. In spite of her practicality, and in spite of the fact she might not want to admit it, for me Chel was one for whom the mystery of life never quite brushes off. Its copper-gold patina increases with age and time. Her size and the birds' were contrasts: two tough boxers in a survival ring. In addition to being born some years before me, Chel was what native folk call an old soul, a soul in a later stage of reincarnation, maybe the fifth rather than the second. I imagined myself to be a young soul. Chel would age faster than I would, owing to the nature of her physique and her work.

With some folk you might turn around, look one day and think, now I know everything there is to know about this person. No more mystery, no surprise. Not Chel. About five summers ago, I caught Chel's reflection in the morning of her summer bath, shaving under her right arm, her arm raised in a sumptuous curve. On an April morning, when Maggie dashed out of the house in a robe to photograph the sunrise, Chel followed her with an umbrella.

I dreamed of Jo last night. She was walking, holding before her own death a small silver lantern. It shone, with one ruby flame in it for the heart. They say that the British speak in order to conceal themselves. I found revelations in a few chosen words at a fish-and-chips place or on a double-decker bus, those scarlets. Jo was remarkable; she seemed both to move under her own free will and to embody a greater, more ironclad will. She had several selves, like Chinese boxes or those crimson Russian egg dolls couched one within another. She embodied the principle of the small perfect version of the will devoted to something larger than the self as one got closer to the core. The smallest, the final doll uncovered at the core would be the most intact, coherent, and radiant of all. There the lens might never slip its nearly soundless click.

Maggie possessed a portrait of Rachel as a child: she stands before a garden chair. In her face is an expression of imminent danger. The wide eyes, the adult brow behind which there are trees swaying. The trees have the density of eighteenth-century painters' trees, which appear to be black or green lace. Some people have a nervous way of avoiding eye contact. Chel met eyes head-on, challenging those who didn't. Like Lewis Carroll, we must all find the key to the garden.

My key was the impetuous stone angels I collected from churchyard discards and granite yards when I was young. Later, my key was the glass lens. Chel has not found her own way, all her own. "Are you drinking more now that we're in England?"

"I'm drinking like a European."

"How's that?"

"Don't you know, Maggie? They like ale at lunch, a stout midafternoon, some wine in the evening." Chel was so frugal that I had to urge her to write out checks to the pharmacist for renewal of the painkiller. The arthritis in her spine was worsening, and she was losing calcium. Was drink a cheaper palliative? The photo I carry of Maggith in my wallet is of her at about thirty, leaning on an elbow at a wooden kitchen table, chin in hand before a steaming cup of coffee. Her face is partially obscured by the steam. I can see the sand running through the hourglass, but the face is younger than I have seen her for years. When the light comes up in the East, I consider Rachel. When the sun goes down, I learn that there are so many layers to the pain of a voluntary separation.

Tonight the sun goes down fast, as it does in winter. Slowly the red satin of the quilted vest runs wine red, as if blood were soaking into it. It is as though my heart had been lanced and blood were pouring out—then all turns black. The widening stain is bright, and then comes night. The red satin of that creature who darted across my sight the other morning and shot again across my retina like a dangling thread came loose and was snapped.

Chel understands the evil and the good in the human heart. She understands how the earth turns. "Rachel's Ramblings" was her column, which she continued from the other side of the Atlantic, but it was about our corner of northern Minnesota, Little Norway. We both enlisted effort toward amnesty, but Chel would thrown down her pen, wrap one hand around the other and say, "After all, Maggie what the hell can we really do?"

"Press on." Neither of us was a slave to time, yet Chel always wore her black watch on her wrist and was clued in to light and the clock after her years and years as mail carrier. I wanted to be free. I wore my maternal grandmother's timepiece on a dark blue velvet ribbon round my neck to use for time exposures.

Light is eloquent: gestures of love and need speak to me. Everything appears threatening at a certain hour close to twilight: seen through rooms of a sunken ship only now discovered by the human eye were shades of blue and eerie gray. Why is the body's desire to be cared for, brought to fulfillment, in a category of its own? Perhaps because like brilliant things, it dazzles.

We packed, hey ho, helter-skelter, to leave London. I could not look back at Big Ben. I felt brine in my eyes. I remember my prayer was divided: if you are there, Lord, keep us as one or let us survive through slow division.

Slow division is terribly long. I have lit a log in daytime, as there is no space heater in my cabin, as in our bed-sitters in England. Playing Renaissance madrigals on a summer morning in Little Norway at our breakfast table, a round wood table painted white. I wanted to capture the circle of the table but could not with my Nikon. "The madrigals are doleful," Chel said. "With a sweet dolefulness," I answered. In August we'd sit cracking eggs, looking for our towhee. In London we had no window in the kitchen. I painted in crude, primitive fashion a window with a vivid red geranium and hung it above the sink. "Our towhee, old bean!" He would come announcing himself, "Tow hee! Tow hee." Polka-dotted, tarty, flouncy tail bobbing, he was a bird like no other.

"Reflections of America" was my life dream. It did not work. Why did it fail? Because it was so damned simple! I had in mind to shoot literal reflections of our small linen factory in the stream or a flock of geese wheeling south in autumn in Brockmorton Lake, a large baronial house in the rich part of Little Norway, and the brick row houses in the poor part compelled me. I traveled from city to city and shot factories, airports, trees, whatever existed near a stream, in order to photograph its reflection. It simply didn't wash. The clarity was there, but my intent was lost. In those days, Rachel went between codeine and the ice pack for her spine. I got mad as a bull and was ready to spit nails about "Reflections of America." My outbursts were never leveled at Rachel but at circumstances that ground us both down. Sometimes she rocked me, "You always bring life home to me." I bought two small Persian carpets. They glowed like stained-glass windows, but even they closed us in on us now. We had explosion after explosion the autumn before I left. All were my doing, the fault of my raw child awaking. Were there indeed that many blowups? Maybe four of what folk would call a scene. Even as they were occurring, draining us of most of our energy, I was able to see them as scenes that could be happening to another twosome. I saw us as figures in a Greek tragedy, playing our roles to the end. There would be catharsis, but there was an underlying ironic question. Why, when age should bring us peace, are we feeling as grating as a dislocated shoulder or hip?

The greenhouse wing, the spark that lit the fire, flowed in its glass over and under all, the wing that was to put out hope, our architectural castle. We'd endured plans for system and pipes, all the small seedlings We'd lived with the smell of wet wood warping. But the structure of our marriage like Peggoty's boat in *David Copperfield*, which Dickens built for Peggoty and his dream children to clamber in on the sands of England. Was it rotting?

Sitting cross-legged on this poor imitation of a bed, while snow crosshatches nightfall, I am able to see the ritual of day, turning clock hands, turning merry-go-round horses when I was a girl, that most ordinary, extraordinary thing. There was no longer room for the circle to come around us that used to protect us at night and lock us like a wedding ring. But, hell, neither of us would wear a ring!

Retirement, if it had unleashed Maggie's savage angel, gave her time for photography. Or were the two one? She worked beyond exhaustion. The price was high. Her prints went more slowly, each seemed to be partially developed in blood. Maggie and Rachel learned that they could be each other's child in great age.

There was an edge to their ardor that no amount of holding, holding on, and holding still could heal. Would Chel go back to breeding sheepdogs? I'm too old, she said. Margaret felt that her life was like a winter feeder to which the most fearless winter birds came. No inner conversations could contain what her few photographs that might live contained. Often, with Chel, she'd wondered how people bore the slowness of life. Something miraculous, then, could strike. Their towhee would come. The globe would hold stock still while the two women looked at him pulsing: a moment of greatness had descended.

Ought they to have bought a new house rather than add a greenhouse? Maggie bit her lower lip and drew blood, spilling it on Chel's old blue work shirt. Harriet was there. They'd fallen to gandering over the dark northern light. It had been an awesome, quick scene. Then it was out: the community, however small and trustworthy, knew, and there was grief.

Then I knew I had to leave. Virginia Woolf walked into the water with a rock tied to her ankle to spare Leonard one more bout of hysteria. My sudden uncontrollable anger, my mood swings; if I could slip away to a world of silver white snow and heal, I might smooth these raw parts that were cutting edges. "The ones we love disappoint us," Chel said, "one way or another." It was bound to be so. She said, "It's the puritan in you, Maggie, that makes you hold on to yourself. Finally you explode."

In New York the second time I shot the longshoremen, docks, snow-covered piers, I dragged Rachel along. I recall a specific Sunday morning shooting the long wharves, hearing great church bells boom down over the Hudson. Rushing down the hills from Riverside Cathedral so like and unlike Little Norway. I wanted the volume of sound recorded in my photos. People were speaking with their hands in French, Italian. They say if you tie a Frenchman's hands, he cannot speak. Despite my reserve, I got down some of their faces. I photographed seagulls; my particular zeal was for making eidetic, italic endangered birds. Rachel too. Some birds lived in Iceland, some as far as New Zealand, some before our very noses at home. When I came to do my book "Women in Prisons," finally I spoke to the human condition. Some were double exposures. Imprisonment, entrapment. Birds could fly over rails, unless they were caged. In some I was able to photograph a bird (sparrow, wren, pigeon) behind the face of a woman. When the book came out, the publisher asked me to write an introduction, but I told him that the photographs were all the introduction required.

Some of the women had the look of one just about to hear the key turn. It is terrible to feel that you are working your way out of bars with one you love. "The British," Chel said, "are great huntsmen. They tether gyrfalcons, you know."

"I know."

"Hawks and hounds." Chel seemed a whole lot more content back in the days when she raised sheepdogs. She needs to do country things. I was more content wearing her dusky wine suede jacket, going to auctions, turning pitchers upside down to scatter the dust out, painting the garage roof, mending the boiler. The thick snowflakes are lit now by my red storm lantern. I like this thick glass. Riding along the richness of earth is the poverty, the poorness of it all: richness being a sleek hound, starvation the poor starved one, all skeletal ribs. Above them all, parallel but above ground, rides the falcon, starkly austere in mastery.

Forty minutes out of London are the green orchards of Kent. A train draws into London, clatters down the track and halts. The sliding door of the luggage car opens, and Chel steps out, "So you've flown one more time, yet I almost beat you. This time you're up from Yorkshire," the husky voice laughs. "And I've taken the damned bumbling train." The station is smoky and noisy. All life seems an accident, but we are together again. She was still the one I most admired, her masked, contained emotion.

I'm not a person for whom the world comes together in morning. It does for Rachel. The world for me often burns together in the setting sun. No icepack on the pond, no bird, no birch bark wrapped in frosty light now. I learn to plot my day around a new set of hours.

Rachel's favorite phrase from Shakespeare would boom out when she banged pots and pants. "It's a great sound and fury, Maggie," she'd claim, "signifying nothing." Smaller sounds signified something. I lie in the total blackness of my cabin, now recalling Bree who was physically able to visualize fear. That fear reflected in her face as though she was looking into a red-hot oven. Bree and Kera, like Cam and Stockard, had fears of their own. Don't we choose what is to frighten us? Only partially. Not as children: real things do stand out there on the horizon, as monumental as the great solar clock Stonehenge. Whenever I feel the power flow through me, I'm overwhelmed. Of what? The light, even of the photos I do not understand. Are women taught to be afraid of the light pouring through them? I remember the crackle of the *Manchester Guardian* and catching Chel's profile above the pages of the paper as we had our morning coffee and scones. "The Limeys have cast- iron stomachs." We reproached ourselves later for not hearing the small comings of disaster, the roll call of our love through the years.

She knocked over the photograph of Josef Karsh, startling Townson. He curled up on Maggie's shoulder and snored until dawn. Morning brought a touch of red through the frosted windowpane. Working the stiffness out of her by moving, Maggie clapped her hands together, started the fire, put the water on to boil. During these morning rituals Maggie continued the imaginary dialogue she'd begun with Jo last midnight: "You are allergic to fireweed, to all flowers, you, who love gardening. You give yourself allergy shots? Do they hurt, you, who had two operations on your spine? Must have been rough to give up caffeine after the second." Maggie focused her lens always back to her shared life with Rachel: in their twenties they'd sit up in bed Friday nights eating great bowls of seafood chowder with big spoons, those two, who were so unlike New England, two old foot soldiers wearing blankets of Payne's gray. Jo had to break the mold of religion before it broke her. I'd come home in my thirties, set up my tripod in our living room, the first small one facing north.

*

"You inspire me when you're inspired," said Chel, "Evenings we spent turning pages of our huge family album." Love as law had a severity that magnetized me. Jo said it was St. Paul who claimed the first law is love. John said all these things in softer terms. She wrestled with the sense that came through black and white's austerity. So much that pleased her in photography pleased her because it made order; it was a statement about human life, but if love had been the first law, how had that law shaken and reshaped her world when she left Rachel to take up a life alone? Was there no such thing as life on one's own?

*

While Rachel in the depth of her night turned questions about love from side to side, Maggie also did in her night. Neither found answers. Each turned the question as a lover does the face. Maggie meditated upon the nights she'd photographed Rachel in Victoria Station, the nights she'd shot Chel in the pool hall bending over the cut, the storm of years riding in her breast, gathering in her eyes, her gray cape flowing. Chel, when she'd had the lump in her breast and biopsy done Friday afternoon came home with lab results. Jo had instructed Maggie, "It's important, Maggie, to give yourself the mind-set that you won't know until the last minute. You're a long-distance runner; you have your energy in control. It had turned out to be benign. Maggie considered her energy in tow; she knew all about the long haul. If she felt herself heading down, she'd have a glass of wine for lunch. What did Rachel take? Chel should go into the clinic for a body rub, give herself some relief for her back. Never would she do that. Instead her anger would detonate like a bomb. Look at your frailties, get some built-in assurances. Hear danger signals. Know them. The wise and grave one's limits. "How do you deal with your anger, Sister?"

"Me, I go out and lash water."

Jo went swimming. Some people knead bread. Cabin fever, the spiritual terror of it all hit Maggie from time to time. She neither lashed water nor kneaded bread. She used the lens. "You love it with too much passion," Jo had said to her once. A spiritual mentor to both of them, Jo saw all sides and knew all truths, it seemed, yet her struggles showed through the flesh. Jo asked Maggie what she did when overwhelmed with emotion. "I curl up and want to die some times."

"That's too passive. That's making yourself into more of a victim than you have to be." "But one wants to relent from effort."

"True." "We can all live under the gun and count down for short amounts of time." It was as though the women heard the whispering of the axe above their heads. "My dreams," said Sister Jo, "always tell me what I need to know." Maggie had taken Jo's hands in hers, hands long and bird-thin, "Jo, why is it the rich who always give the least?" "That's how they stay rich." Jo had a wonderful fading glamour.

Sometimes Jo had a chalk-on-blackboard face, and Maggie smiled when she saw the women with whom Jo had sewn hems all those years in the convent. That is the way you move, old darling.

So during their time in England, at night Maggie had checked her watch and saw Rachel moving on the late night train coming into Victoria Station in London from Folkestone in Kent.

Once is not enough for life. I want it over again. Chel said to me angrily, "The toilet seat's broken. I just got a splinter."

"Let it slide." Can't let the toilet seat slide." I want the ice of a
February morning, I want to go back to the beginning, when we
were playful, sticking icicles to each other's tongues as we scrape the
windshield.

The law was love. With that in hand, you needed no other. The
law was also light. Light coming through the lens was fractured into a
greater light. John Donne said that good is as visible as green. Maggie
was elected Most Distinguished Graduate of the high school. "What do
you think of my suit?" she'd asked Rachel on the brink of the occasion.
Rachel leaned back and frowned. "Dyed it myself," Maggie blurted. "To
take the measure of a human being is no mean task," said Helga, "A
large human being can bring off such a suit," Maggie had said to Rachel.
"Remember," she'd asked Rachel on the drive over, "the magic-lantern
shows when were kids?"

"Yes." Maggie also remembered that the first month in the cabin
was as cold as Japan. "I am in a black hole," she'd warned Rachel, while
driving over to the opening of one exhibition in Little Norway. "You've
been deep down before, Maggie. I have great faith in your power to pull
yourself up by your bootstraps." No boots, no straps was how she felt.
Yet they'd chatted more about magic lanterns, while the spring rain
transformed the woods outside Little Norway into a Pierre Bonnard or
a Manet painting, as though the woods themselves were seen through a
magic lantern. The increasing demands on Maggie to speak floored her;
she felt awkward. Her voice would come up like a child's at the bottom
of a well. Somewhere near the end of the talk, she'd be given a second
wind. Her voice came from somewhere deeper inside her; her voice took
on weight and was resonant like Chel's. Racing to the home gate, she'd
become the high-strung, articulate creature she was.

At last tonight a thick, full winter snow fell over the whole country
outside the cabin. It was Kawabata's Japan, a photograph as sharp as
Euclid. Now, snow covered both lens and love's laws. When she dreamed
that night, Maggie saw the small lights of cities, crosshatching lights in
a steel plant, the glowing grids of cities from a plane, Milwaukee was it?
Or Chicago? In New York during her exhibitions, she and Rachel used
to take cabs. Chel was tough enough to match the old cabbies. She spoke
a kindred tongue, a cigarette dangling from her unpainted lip. Through
it all I admired her calm stoicism. We two were whisked along by a force,
like so many leaves in autumn back to solitude, our twosome. We were
the shadows of two women moving into a certain geometry, frontier
spirits. No longer struggling to prove myself as artist, wasn't I struggling
to stay alive? I didn't want my sleep to come from a bottle. Sleeplessness
carved into her energies. She dreaded the paper boy's coming at five a.m.,

slinging the paper at their front stoop while the first birdcalls signaled
that the day itself must turn on its great revolving wheel once more.

That last year when they slept in separate rooms, she'd hear Chel
sigh down the hall. Burleson, growing restless, pawed the rug. The dog
found the new sleeping arrangement strange, but he always slept beside
his master, Chel: a one-woman dog nosing about in the tool shed, in
the bedroom, doing woeful things. Rachel was heavy yet graceful rising.
Down the rabbit hole of dream. They were taking a dream ferry ride.
They reached the destination of a long journey, boarded on the back of
a ferry, where they were closed in a dark room, a sort of battle stall with
no light around. The other passengers had a view until slowly, slowly a
wood slat slid open and she and Rachel caught a glimpse of sky, a gold-
red sunset flooding the spun steel of one of the nation's great bridges,
perhaps the George Washington, defining the black silhouette of the Big
Apple. I loved her most deeply when I was preparing to leave. Could that
be possible? After the knock-down, drag-out in front of Harriet when
she called me on my unquiet ways? Her family were clergy people. What
was my father? A poor woodcarver. Warped like a faulty old mirror on
a merry-go-round, one of those brought over from Europe, I must leave,
revolving now, slow and forgotten in the rain.

I was pushing the envelope, daring to explore the frontier of solitary
living in old age. Mentally packing, I saw people inside railway carriages
in photographs I'd taken. These faces were charged with urgency, driven
by tragedy or exile, they traveled by rail. Were they called to a funeral, a
wedding? Some of the faces were hardened as though with a varnish of
grief, northbound-facing, holding on for a kind of eternity.

Flash! My domineering beloved, I am flying nude through the yard,
on a dare streaking with a red feather duster. I see sun flares, which are
my bane. I see mother stepping into stark foreverness against the stark
Minnesota prairie heaven.

*

Maggie woke to a snowstorm. Crystal by crystal, it had built up in her
cabin window. She wanted to write Chel but had run out of stamps. As
particle after particle of light forms a face in a photograph, so stroke after
stroke of words of thought formed in her mind. As grain after grain of
light is swallowed into darkness, so were her morning impulses; in late
day the hand would not obey the heart. So began a new vision. There
was a hard white moon like a bullet. Just as the towhee was printed
on Maggie's mind, so was were the cherry tree and stone angel. These
were Maggie's North Star being printed to infinity like old copperplate
negatives in an endless sequence in her eye.

Later, in her forties, standing against the garden, Margaret knew they'd got life down, she and Rachel. Birds make nests, the fox lays his head, but the daughter of woman, where has she? O my darling, the frustration the flesh. When afternoon is laid out like ivory in a lacquer box, all points shining. I try to find the angle for the whole vision. I try to commit betrayals of the affordable kind: photographing a human face maintaining privacy. I violently oppose color and stick to my black and white but am constantly seeing life in color that is translatable into blacks, whites, silvers. Chel, in your tattered coat and leather gloves, you know photography is a magnet to my steel. My light meter does what it can; the requirements of love change. A face stripped can move more into its own.

It crossed Maggie's mind to drive down to the church in Little Norway. Trudy and she always left during the final hymn on Sunday so that they could get their bikes out before the crowds. She still went with Rachel to the Church of Our Lord, the oldest in Little Norway. Why did Maggie continue to go? Rachel had quit years ago. Was Chel the stronger for having been a twin, once identical in the womb, then after birth with hands locked? Mystical, the revenant of Dolly haunted her. Like the two shadows of the horse in the field Chel saw when she was ten, they were spirituality and psychology entwined, nearly one. In steel colors tonight Maggith read the whole earth's horizon. Like a bell tolling. "Your hoarding ways," Chel had claimed last October, "have come between us." The image of herself as ungenerous unhinged Maggie. After, she brought Chel pots of boiling tea the way Janet Clay liked them. When Rachel accused her of being ungenerous, Maggie was so riled she could go out and shoot a porch light. But she had no porch, no light. Tonight, recalling this, she went out and shot great lashings of snow; she learned new things, such as the way silver hit a bead of light like mercury in a pan of soaking water. What would that be like? A cluster of bright flannels like flags flashed through her mind. The wallpaper she and Rachel once had in the dining room had dense purple flowers that closed when they dreamed. These in turn derived from the nightgowns she slept and dreamed in as a child. Do I want to start counting years backwards, to be a kid again in a gingham dress and saddle oxfords that smelled of shoe polish? A first day in spring or autumn? Yes, autumn! I carried my raisiny smelling pencil case that held the Eberhard Faber eraser that I liked to bend back and then let it snap straight.

Why did I leave so close to Christmas? St. Olaf's phoned when their teacher was ill. I had been restless for a long time. I thought Christmas festivities would provide some consolation for Chel, at least distractions. Rachel would be among our community; I was the one who would be going it alone. Weary, I had still to be moving. To go through Christmas rituals when the heart in me was dead over it would have been to die twice.

Chapter Sixteen

An Iridescent Quality

She had handed the letter from St. Olaf's to Sister Jo, who read it and smiled up at Maggie, "Where is the warmth coming from?"

"I don't know."

"They want you; it's clear. Just look at that faded typewriter ribbon."

Chel kept returning to her with a slow yearning, like Renaissance tunes for flutes. Maggie dreamed she was teaching a course to folk who were learning to become postal carriers. She had to teach them how to unlock boxes, carry sacks of mail. A big black dog sat at her feet thumping the floor with his tail as she lectured.

Townson looked at wrens nearly frozen on the branch but breathing. Something in Maggie had perhaps frozen at the age of ten. After her mother left earth, abandoning her as a child, Maggie cultivated her imagination until it was as lush as an Elizabethan garden. Her mama went into black and white; a frosted earth lay over her, above her a frozen heaven. Turned to marble. Was marbleized a word, the child asked? Yes, of course, it had all turned, her outlook on life upon her mother's early death. She wilted like a fruit on the vine before her Aunt Cornelia's eyes.

Those were long evenings when she and Chel had played the game of kings in a winter kitchen with torn sky-blue linoleum. Who would put in sky-blue linoleum? Was Chel, with the more formal religious background, aware that her lover, as she lifted the king, also feared leaving? "I've castled your queen."

"So you have," Chel would look up and smile concession, her mole-gray glasses case in her hip pocket. Then Chel would rise and bang the kettle on. Car lamps were turning on miles below in town tonight. Twenty miles below lay civilization. The fish-blue eyes of televisions seemed to revolve, standing in one place, twirling globes. The old black-and-white tellys reminded Maggith of cockaded ptarmigan. Meals would be cooking, chatter and quarrel in kitchens, banter and hugging. She suddenly saw an ambulance with a red cross marked ADVANCED CARE UNIT flash by. It halted at a red light in the blizzard; it could not proceed with its ill person, as snow whirled in its headlamps. Civilization.

Maggie's one friend who came to the cabin was a map maker of the Lake Regions. Ellen's mother was Estonian, her father Finnish. Ellen Pareve was forty-one, young enough to be a daughter. In the cabin she typed on the old Underwood, the ribbon faded like the one on the letter which St. Olaf's had sent her last year. Another black-and-white thing she liked was ribbon. "Dear Ellen, my coffee with you is my one bow in the direction of civilization. Perhaps you will drive back with me next week to the cabin."

I still belong to another. What if I were to come back like the prodigal and be refused entrance?

By nightfall what she observed out the cabin window was a dense frieze of snow like fustian. She drew on Chel's old black woolen stockings.

I see the box of white tissues by our large Norwegian bed, the two bright blue water cups, one on either side. How strange last year was: one bed, one water cup, two rooms. Your people, Chel, conform. My folks tend to reform. I see the design of a Pennsylvania quilt sewn circa 1860 with dark green leaves blocked on it. Surrounded by piles of unfinished work, I see that which was finished was done with extreme care.

Maggie's inner life had been like a geode: plain on the outside but, once cracked open, it revealed gleaming color. Maggie's inner life revealed its secrets to few, perhaps none. Life should hold an iridescent quality. She wanted to do a series of contemporary women that surpassed the young women she'd photographed in the tuberculosis sanatorium in 1947 to illustrate tenacity, energy, and courage defined in their lean bone format. "The San" it was called. Some critics called her morbid, but it was a social statement. She came in for criticism over that portfolio, but it won the prize for best portfolio by a Minnesotan that year. She captured in the faces of these girls under sixteen the will power it takes to keep alive all winter watching only the birds and looking for signs of changing colors in the snow, portents of spring, when you're not sure at all spring will come. Renaissance. Iridescence. She turned the words around in her mind. Could one reclaim a lost childhood?

Maggie was beyond the age when people sort out major things, when they remarry. That was for the middle period of life. I am old, she thought, yet I am grafting. I never had a sister and always wanted one. But Chel's hand is in mine: when apple trees come out like girls in tulle in spring, her hand moving before the oriental quail and the cockaded quail. In many faces I see the ravages of God and want to capture that wrestling. How can I whisper to the man in the moon words like "quiet candle maker, calendar turner." I yank on my boots and step outside. Crunch goes the thick frost on old snow. You go out into the woods and the monster turns into a unicorn. I scan the night sky for the mathematics of our journey, but there are no stars tonight. Jo is a pincushion armed with God, as the sky is often with stars. Do I pray?

"I've a strange thing to tell you, Maggie," Jo said one day. "I was raised by a male mother."

"How?"

"When I was two years old, mother had her first nervous breakdown. Her strength gave out, and she was rearing the four of us in the wilderness. Then father took over; he changed me, fed me, took us down to the Mojave Desert and taught me to sing. I was taught gentleness by him."

In London's first blackout, a few cars threading streets with lights on, the first great evacuation. The analogies between Maggie's leaving Rachel and the war flooded Chel again and again then stopped abruptly at the end of calm.

It's good to keep your oar in; you turn in circles if you use only one. The other shore shone with pinpoints of light like a small dock where a Japanese fishing boat was landing in early evening.

Chapter Seventeen
It's Venison, My Love

For Rachel's fiftieth birthday, Maggie had taken her to a quietly elegant restaurant, The Chalet. What they'd eat was to be a surprise. Maggie phoned ahead, told the cook what Chel liked and left it up to him. She liked almost everything. "Serve us your best," she admonished him. Those were the times, the times when love made no demands because it had met them. They sat by the window, and Rachel poured her favorite wine: rich, thick, dark gold Hungarian Tokay. She had scanned the sky, "It's a night with stars." Indeed, dense stars glittering above as the waiter poured the wine. Chel's dusky laughter turned heads in the small restaurant. In the blazing fireplace fat logs crackled, and a smoked-glass mirror reflected the scene. The waiter brought the main course. Rachel gasped, "It's venison, my love!" Chess, the game of kings; horse racing, the sport of kings; venison, the food of kings. Venison, gamey and rich and dark, tasted of the woodiness that was Rachel. Chel said with another glass of Tokay, "When you grow up with wild water, you want a bit of wild water every now and again. I dearly love mountains, my Maggie, and need them nearby, but water ..." and she waved toward one of the inlets that form the great Boundary Waters outside the dining room window. She waved, then let her arm drop back, and sighed with satisfaction. It was a non sequitur, but she said she used to stand on the mudguard of the car when she was young and went whizzing along. "You didn't."

"Oh, but I did," she said, leaning forward, reaching for a cigarette. Venison wasn't light, but it positively floated compared to the shepherd's pies they'd got back in London. Both the meat and fish pies went down like a lead sinker. The colors of the room were handsome as a peacock's tail. Chel spoke of her past, whose richness unrolled itself like an Oriental carpet. "It's terrific," she flushed, "going downhill. Not all like a push bike."

At her fiftieth birthday it seemed her history was a net that snared the wild ptarmigan. They turned to discussing puppeteer Helga, "Can you imagine," Maggie asked, leaning forward, "tossing up each day between life and death? Having to decide each dawn to live all over again?" "No, nor living totally alone. I couldn't live alone and face that sort of dilemma."

Yet each of them now was doing just that thing. That was what gave Helga courage. With cancer, she took each day and made it a work of art. She'd done pottery for years; now her puppets portrayed her soul as though she carved in their wooden faces the ravages of God. Chel had been at her best, at the top of her game, at her fiftieth. Always chief cook and bottle washer, always guardian of the meals, she had relaxed. The mirth often held at bay by her large body and staunch mind relaxed, became almost Falstaffian, with a touch of iridescence poured like golden honey, or the Tokay itself, flowing over the scene, fixing it for Margaret in a varnish as lustrous as an old master's painting.

Chapter Eighteen
Gone Canoeing

When the lake was fire-rimmed with the sun rising, the two women
would go down early, put one oar in the water, and shoot grass with dew
as bright as ice. They'd go see the cygnets. As they'd walked back arm
in arm, Rachel had thought that life draws a tighter circle. They left the
swans glad of the fact that Maggie's camera was back at home. This was
so intimate a scene that the camera must not record it. Waters parted like
silver mercury divided by the wind knife behind them. It was late spring.
Endurance breathed side by side. Later, in a red flare of quilted fire, Chel
had seen the night light up. "It's worth a look, darling. Come."

No one took a photograph of us together during our last two years.
The untaken photograph was developed in my eyes as if that image
distilled loss and love. Maggie had a vision she tried to blot out. Rebecca,
a first cousin, one of six on a farm on the Boundary Waters, had knit
an end bitterer even than Chel's twin, Dolly. She'd been out riding in a
horse and team with her brothers and sisters. The horses panicked and
pulled apart in opposite direction. The T-stick went up in the air and
sent Rebecca flying up. When she came down, she landed right on the
stick; she was shafted, impaled.

War bond images subside. Chel could be impossible before breakfast.
Maggie wore a tunic that could have been worn in a stage play about St.
Joan. Jo knew, when she wore the habit, that beyond the brick walls it
was spring. Something cleared a hedge, rippled over the grass as silently
as the canoes rippled over water, then was shot, running.

Chapter Nineteen
Sleep Like a Child Under Your Needs

During the winter when Rachel burned her arm, Maggie thought about going into nursing. She found herself surprisingly adept. That was the winter the two of them had fallen in love with the boy Petré. He had multiple birth defects: born blind and spastic, he spoke in fits and starts, his hands trembled. These traits brought the world and its message to him in a special way. He was a monkey wrench to adopt the orphanage said.

Maggie yanked on red gloves, went out and stomped, brushed, and scraped huge chunks of ice off the outside of the cabin. She still heard her stirred-up voice from the night. What is love but a chain of memories? Am I hiding away like the child who wishes to be found?

During the winter she had been sick, Chel's nature shone through like a brass sun through flesh. I wanted to live forever in that position on my back so that my lungs didn't hurt. Then I'd feverishly rip off blankets, bull that I was, Taurus. I came to know that the longest hours are the hours when you are boxed in. I had to be up and about, roaming, rising on my elbow, hair plastered to my forehead from fever. "I want to scrub the scrub basin." "The basin will wait."

"Who do you think you are, my turnkey?"

Maggie sat in on a glass-blowing class this afternoon. She thought of those early days when she had left her aunt and shared a cold-water apartment with three other girls. She scraped the bottom of the barrel only to get a splinter. With the help of her high school art teacher, Mrs. Todis, she put together a portfolio, and she won a partial scholarship. Scholarships were hard to land on the heels of the Depression unless a girl enrolled in agricultural college and learned to drive a tractor while pursuing a Ph.D. in Latin or English. Chelsea, a woman she knew in her twentieth year, did precisely that and copped highest prizes for top grades to boot. Maggith drove the jeep for her uncle who started a business on the side called North Minnesota Recovery. On his truck Mag painted MINERAL & METAL DETECTION NEEDS and his phone number. What an odd time driving up hill, down dale like the soldier boys. After the war, she had enough money to enroll in a female normal school, as teaching schools were horridly misnamed in those days, and majored in art education. She breathed a sigh of relief when she left waitressing. When she arrived at St. Olaf's college with a cardboard valise, she was stunned by its plainness, which as almost grim. Later visiting industrial cities, where the linen mills stand in northern England, she saw the same leaden sky and shale she had seen at St. Olaf's. What had taken her this route? The desire to leave home to pursue her own life, of course. She took an evening course in darkroom techniques, and this was the love of her life. Art was her legal marriage, photography her inspiration.

The fate-filled evening she met Chel was burned into her memory. They literally bumped into each other in the library stacks. Rachel had been training to become a reference librarian.

I was turning in circles all that winter. I was taken. I had my first smash on a woman, my first realizable one. Chelsea had been a spark, a fire out of my reach. I worked my butt off. My teeth went to hell that winter. I had trench mouth. When I lost most of my teeth in my early thirties, Chel took it quietly as a reserved person does. She pulled on her black coat to go out one night in December, and said "I'd do anything to help you hold on to them, old bean." I sold photographs of graveyard angels but not enough to pay for dental work. My angels looked as if their wings were stone, which they were. I lost some teeth to decay but gained darkroom techniques. So there we were, apart seven years that spanned a war, which shook and reshaped the world. If we are all prisoners of love and of our bodies, we can see through a chink in the pavement, the light of the world, which shines up, and see through a hole in the top of the sky. Seven years apart, Chel and I were what is called a Jacob's age, separated in years when we met round the corner of a stack in that small college town. When the head librarian came around, did it look as though there'd been a bit of a dust-up? Chel was vigorously pulling down volumes of forgotten history, blowing dust out of them, which hit the librarian in the face. All this occurred by the light of dim bulb as yellow as a mosquito bulb, no gold dome of Christopher Wren. It was a clue to Chel's historical orientation that she haunted the library. Chel was up on a high ladder that evening and nearly fell backward when she learned the librarian had gone to the same high school we had. I'd been told it. Chel said the words were just ringing in her ears. Her alto voice stirred me through the soles of my shoes. The earth rocked. I toughed it out, but I was in her ken from then. "You look like a hawk, a small blond hawk," Chel said from above. Chel's outfits then were tailored and a bit severe.

Shaking off the ice with a shudder like a small bear, Maggie stomped back into the cabin, fed Townson some milk, and gave the reluctant fire a poke. She'd decided to treat herself this morning: scrambled eggs with a knob of butter melted in the pan. She needed energy if she was to battle the car down into town. She felt she was St. Joan in her tunic going forth to meet the Dauphin. She might have to spend the night with Ellen if the storm worsens. Ellen had maps all over her small rooms. They thrust forth where the earth had thrown up mountains, dipped where the earth-gouged lakes sank in. These maps captured both silence and sound. Milk teeth from Ellen's sixth winter were in a little cardboard box by the bed. When Chel's mother was dying, Maggie concluded, it was the child in me, my girl child, who needed to be held in loving arms again. Now I have my own exile. Maggie hadn't stormed out. She'd sat down and enumerated grief wishes for change. Struggling, they had drawn up verbal lists: what to do about Karyn, the greenhouse, possessions, friends. Telling them and giving this a trial run. The plants waiting to germinate in boxes, seedlings in the iron bitter cold of the year were safe.

"Rachel, I'd like to take a season alone."

"I wouldn't choose," Chel labored, hard of breath, "the dark of year. Not right now after your birthday and with Karyn sick.

They were in the kitchen, where their scenes invariably occurred. They held summit meetings of the heart and both dreamed the peaceful setting of an Arthurian round table.

"You want to spend a season alone?" Rachel sat back down.

"A season, yes" she repeated the word that was beginning to lose its meaning.

"I see," Rachel said gravely.

"I need the challenge of seeing if I can teach this photography course," Maggie summed up.

Chel swung out the flask of brandy. When Maggie wrote Chel to tell her that she was teaching a second term, it had seemed natural. Karyn used to say to her daughter, Rachel, "You've made your bed, now sleep in it, child." But Chel could not sleep. She was no child.

Helga, when her eyes exactly met yours, conveyed a strange courage, but she often wore her mask. Maggie crossed the border up into Canada once with Helga but most often with Rachel: border guards in uniform leaped menacingly out at night with their scarlet flares throwing fire into the face. Was that why Maggith always associated fear with borders?

It is always difficult to live with another; it is always tricky to traverse a border. Maggie decided to stay with Ellen. She didn't want to spend the night alone with the dogs of her imagination. The storm cracks branches; roofs threaten to cave in. She thought about the six-pointed star that framed their lives: Chel, Maggie, Jo, Harriet, Helga, and the boy Petré.

Although Chel never became a librarian, her idea of having died and gone to heaven was spending a Saturday in the library. She often came home laden with books about wildflowers, potting, planting. Books on cooking, canoeing, the Boundary Waters came in too. Maggie was a sponge, soaking up all inspirations in life. Colors were crushed, heaped, here in the northlands. There was the six-pointed star and the eight-pointed star. The six-pointed star was the star of David. There were evenings of Chel's stamp collecting, laying out many colored stamps, first-day issues.

She pictured Chel without her: a setting in which she had never seen her lover. Self-authorship is ironic. Ironically, each woman survived on inner dialogue. When the face is scarred, what is changed? Often the expression is altered. That night at Ellen's Maggie drew out the latest letter and read it word by word, her finger tracing the cursive. Why should I not sell our home since I am in debt and no longer need such a home alone? It was not large, but it did us fine.

With no electricity in the cabin, only kerosene, and no telephone, she encountered the last demons of age: physical hardship and isolation. Yet she felt a certain calm and astringent clean as boiled water was poured into the pan. Saturday night was bath time. Each woman had needed her own carrel, Maggie decided closing her eyes in the tub she recalled one of Chel's saying at the post office taped to her carrel: "Behold the turtle. Was she like one of Roman Vishniac's children of a vanished world? Going into this willed exile in great age had rounded out to a year and a month. Maggie managed to fall into sleep like a child under the needs and commands of a body bathed and warmed.

She felt a surge of vitality as she swung up from the tub, where she'd leaned back on her haunches, like a crouching child. The strength comes from the shoulders. Maggie drew on layers of clothing: flannel nightgown, robe, sleeping socks. She knew Chel did the same. She didn't know about the fact Chel wore the star quilt as a cape. Star was icon. She ran a towel through her short hair. She'd cut it like a boy's. "Good night, then, Ellen," Maggie came to the darkened door of Ellen's bedroom. "Good night, Maggie," Ellen said. She turned in early. Maggie crawled into the bed down the hall, feeling the strangeness of sleeping in a bed again. She heard the odd car swish by through the snow on the crest. Town sounds. She felt scrubbed of emotion. Chinese sages say they begin to know at age eighty-five.

PART THREE

Beside a Flickering Blue Flame
"Her Lady's ta'en another mate . . ."

Walker Evans at a comparatively early age found himself possessed of a vision of America, a sharp insight into its grandness and sadness, its awful dreariness, and its lyric, redemptive simplicity.
—Lloyd Fonvielle,
The Aperture History of Photography Series, #12

In London one never hears an airplane. The sky is quiet, patrolled only by blimps, which glitter in the sunlight like swollen fairy elephants lolling against the blue.
—Mollie Panter-Downes, London War Notes

Chapter Twenty
The Letters

When I see wild animals move against darkness, I think of you: the deer who occasionally come up to the edge of the cabin and nibble frost in autumn. Leaves in spring remind me of you. I am drunk on memory. In a thin, child's voice, I cry out. Who now shares my glacial view of fields. Today I saw a teal-blue sky against white tombstone branches and thought color could have done it better. In my solitude, this is a kiss.

The hunchback and the wren. That's what I saw when I posed with Chel once: she was doubled over with pain.

Back from Ellen's, Margaret moved around restlessly in her cabin the following morning. By two p.m. she had found it necessary to light the oil lantern, which at first was smoky. She turned the wick down to a clear yellow. Now it was burning right. Ellen kept her distance, chatting over steak and red wine. She kept a distance, as though she sensed the presence of graying and respected the distance imposed between two people. Blue invaded everything: from granite cinderblocks to wood logs outside in the shed for burning. Maggie had seen Sister Jo's face, a thin face on a thinner body, her right leg a full two inches shorter than her left, which made her spine an "S." She was born this way. Just as the star of David, made of two triangles, was born with six points, the pivotal people in her life were six. When the wild animals stirred, moving against darkness, she saw the star quilt. During their very last days together last December, Maggie had thought Chel looked strikingly handsome. "You know you're stinkingly out of sorts," Rachel had wheeled around and handed it to her. "You're right. I am. Time I was moving on." In the stillness of a house surrounded by freshly fallen snow, the words had flown. The snow was imitation purity, an imitation of intense quiet. Maggie had flung the window open on the heels of Rachel's having banged it down.

"I consider that swift," Maggie protested.

"I don't know that word," Chel said.

"Unreal, Rachel."

"When you cut me down, use words I know," Maggie raised her voice.

Margaret was recalling that once you've passed through purgatory in Dante's hell, it's clear sailing. But she wasn't sure those were her visions. She was not a Catholic. Under the low starry sky outside the cabin, Margaret took up her pen, an old quill, and dipped it in ink. She felt like a schoolgirl in a woodcut of the schoolchild in Iowa that Karyn had bequeathed her. She felt she was the hound who had gone hunting. She

wanted her hawk to bring her home. Chel had called her hawk, however.
She wrote in light of the flickering oil lantern:

Dear Rachel,
You have a Biblical name. When I think about you, I see a woman
with Biblical patience. Tonight I can see Jo's face before me. I could not
sleep. I am troubled in my mind. There is much I must explain to you
that I was unable to in the hurry and shock of leaving. I want to let you
know, if I am able to, what strange feelings moved in me. Now I live in a
snow world. My isolation is almost total. I see that I have steadily pushed
myself back further up against isolation. Yet here I am. I find myself on
the verge of writing you a love letter, but how dare I?
Yours, Maggie

*

Maggie looked at the small mirror, a mere rectangle, leaning against a
wood candleholder on the writing table. She did not know the woman in
the glass. Her face had altered in these thirteen months, a baker's dozen.
Her skin looked as silvery and fine as talc in this eerie light. It was more
leathery and weathered than when she'd left. I have aged ten years in
one, she laughed at herself. Night was awesome. She was shrunken. The
lantern showed wide-set eyes, more black than green but still seafaring
in this unsteady flame. The wide mouth was capable of humor. She
shrugged. Her shoulders ached.

So it was that the second batch of love letters began. The first were
mailed the summer they were separated, after they had fallen in love
almost four decades ago.

Chapter Twenty-one
Rachel Reads

A block of sun hit Rachel's icebox, lit it up like a cake of white ice glowing in late afternoon. To the right of the fridge was the cork bulletin board where she had fixed scrawled notes with pushpins : MATCHES & BUTTER. She had been reading M. F. K. Fisher's *The Art of Eating.* She'd binged on some small Japanese rice cookies that Jo had given her. Looking out the kitchen window at the snow, Chel recalled building snow forts, having fights as a child, fisticuffs. The block of sun faded. Small blessings.

She'd fired up the big brick oven. Last night she had taken Helga's long hand in hers. Helga's hand felt sculptural, finely carved, thin-boned and strong. Earlier Chel had sat with Janet Clay through dinner. "I'm making reasonable sense of my widowhood. How do you manage, Rachel?"

"I do, I manage," Rachel had said. She relived the conversation, running her fingers though Burleson's neck ruff. "It was January, you know, when we married. I always had cold hands. That makes me a good pastry cook," said Chel. "You married him for his warm hands."

"You could say I did," said Janet. That was back in England before the war. Later Janet had come out as a woman's woman in subdued fashion like the rose and teal of her embroidered flowers. She kept a low profile.

"Darling," said the note that years ago Maggie had propped up on the sugar bowl, "please don't throw away these petals floating in the bowl. I want to photograph them. I'm making a sachet." The note was now folded in Rachel's pocket under her cape.

And to think people said that you just photograph. You just open a vein and shoot a picture was how Maggie felt about it. Janet had enlarged upon her solo life: "I can still concoct a meal these days, despite my weak eyes, but have no appetite. The doc gave me a tonic, saying I'm ordering you a woman to talk with during your supper." "Dandy," Rachel said. "Nice thing it is to have company."

"I'm old, Rachel. I pray the Lord will come in the night. Like lucky Mandy: one day I dropped in, and she looked as though she had been embroidering and had fallen asleep over her colors. When I touched her, she was there no more."

"Janet, you're a going concern."

"You don't have to pay. I will come!"

"No, I will eat alone, but keep me company tonight. I bought a cottage roll." Famished for food and talk, the two women fell to the meal. These were the requirements of love. Janet spoke about the great train robbery, the Victorian era, the concept of the criminal. Before her ancient lace curtains, she talked to Chel, her hand trembling as she lifted the china cup with rose flowers painted on it to her lip. Rachel, walking home, saw Helga thinner, elfin. Helga, like several in the community, was harried, hurried, fighting for time, buying time. Helga's hands had dropped into darkness and left Janet Clay's face rising proud into widowhood.

Helga dropped by Rachel's for coffee with a touch of brandy laced that they took at the kitchen table. Nothing particularly romantic, but Rachel had reached across the Bering Strait of imagination, the kitchen table, and taken Helga's hand. They held hands a long time. Rachel could feel her chapped cheeks blushing. She rose, indicating an end to the evening.

When she came home from a walk with Burleson, Chel found a letter from Margaret. A landslide of bills was the common thing. She felt tension rise in her throat and reached for the pack of cigarettes she had stashed in the lower desk drawer. A cold wind was whipping the trees. She had no curtains to draw. She looked at the red-and-white-painted Swedish horse in her memory.

FIRST LADY OF CRIBBAGE read the inscription on the gold-plated trophy that Janet Clay had won. Now where would the trophy live? It as odd the way the same symbol, a sitar, gleamed high in the northern afternoon, odd the way the same symbol turned up in various places, a haunting repetition of pattern. Chel moved on a razor edge of decided living, yet its edge was anguish. Another war. The year turned, showing its Janus face, January, the month for looking both forward and backward.

She looked down at the cigarette, the nicotine staining her nails yellow, and stubbed it out with a vengeance. Her own letters to Maggie had been few and far between. It felt strange to send letters after years of delivering and sorting them, after years of breathing side by side. She sat for a long time, staring into the small, gray, narrow light of their north-facing kitchen. It was still theirs. Then leaning upon the table, she rose in her moth-eaten gray cardigan, drew on her windbreaker, and decided to take a long walk with Burleson.

People talk about living other lives; this one was all she could fathom. She and Maggie had led a calm, regular life, as circular as clockwork. It is true: one opened a vein and wrote, bit the bullet, and took a photograph or a decision. The days were long, but the years were short. Their shared life had been like the boat traveling from shore to shore, jagged if looked at close up but making a straight path in the end. At times Maggie smoked as though she was drinking the cigarette. Rachel feared cancer next to death. She took a long walk to get the matches and butter. She left the burner on blue with the coffee pot atop it. She left an uneaten biscuit on her plate as she yanked down the jacket from the hall nail. The jacket was crumpled, the nail bent. She walked past Christ Church, gray as steel in the cold. They were teaching a gymnastics class for young children; she could see the agile bodies of four- and five-year-old girls and boys tumbling. Janet had no mirror; her eyes were gone. Chel, "I can't sleep—that's my problem."

This was extreme age: staring into the dark became a kind of light, knowing not what would come but that death was certain and life uncertain. The past year had seen a toughening to Rachel's language, a harshness to its idiom that she had noticed, then put down to solitude. It was more suitable to a generation of people younger than she was. Yet such phrases as "messing up" and "slamming out the door" came to her tongue.

Coming clean. That was the phrase that kept coming to her mind as she strode through the snow, clean snow and old snow mixing together. Slow to respond verbally, Chel had imagined an answer to Maggie's letter. "Now, Maggie, you know me. I got your letter, but words come slowly, so don't worry if word doesn't come for a while." She went in the door to Karlson's grocery for the matches and butter. She tossed in a bag of chocolate chip cookies. "You look as if you'd been to hell and back," said old Karlson. "Yes," she said. The power of an electric bulb to flood a room was striking. Old Karlson had his ceiling light burning. No shade. He never bothered. In this Arctic dark of late afternoon, the bulb was a small fierce sun burning. Rachel glanced up and smiled back at the floor. She walked home with a lope. The coffee was burned. She began the letter while reheating stew for supper. Jo phoned and asked, "Feeling stouter?"

"Some," Rachel said with caution, "I'm working at it."

Was she having what historians call a crisis of conscience? What was happening to her mind? It was cracking open like an India rubber ball: black inside. Janet Clay says in dream, "It would please me to see my dress, although I cannot pick out my face." Rachel felt heavy. Jo was her right wing, Maggie her left. Without both how could she fly? She felt as earthbound as the woolens she wore today.

Dear Maggie,

I got your letter. I am being obliged to uncover and discover a new vision of our connections through solitude. Your letter gives me a sense of how you are living now. I remember the times you write about. We climbed together inside the safety deposit box, and you were taken aback by all that silver in the ancient boxes.

You ask how I am managing. I do well enough. All about me in our community I see folk sinking out of solitude. Some fall into a state close to death, I believe. Some fall into depression. I want you to continue your exploration of whatever wilderness you have chosen. I hope you do more portraits.

For myself, I am careful with my feelings. It has been a year as high as a mountain and as deep as a canyon. I do not suppose two old birds who know each other so well as you and I do need many words. The house is cold, even the kitchen. I use a space heater sometimes. I am taken by surprise and of course am delighted when you speak of wanting to return home in spring. Will there be a home? What can I say until you are certain.

Yours, Rachel

She picked up the phone and dialed with care. "Jo, I heard from Maggie today. She thinks of coming home in spring."

As sure as God's in Gloucestershire, Chel thought of the little green apples when they rang off. She was smiling. As sure as God made little green apples, she and Margaret belonged together. She closed her eyes, then opened them, and laughed out loud. Impatient as a girl of seventeen. You go into another country for love every time. Have I even begun to master the treacherous technique of living alone? Absently, Rachel picked up her father's gold pocket watch from the bedside table. She was reminded of Maggie's photo of the silver clock in the darkened bedroom. Just the clock ticking, outlines picked out in mercury silver. For the longest time it had not worked right. Then it began again.

She had shared the space in her mother's body with Dolly. With Maggie she had shared her life on earth. "Love shouldn't affect you so drastically," said the old Lutheran grandmother inside her, but Rachel threw open the covers to the stamp album tonight spraying dust about the kitchen. Burleson had a sneezing fit. She herself sneezed five times. She felt she had walked out the door old this morning and returned to a second youth this afternoon. After all, when her youth was done, what had she to show for it?

I was a woman who needed a child. Out of our union many were born. Maggie, too, is a mothering woman, despite having had scant mothering herself. What will we do if she returns. I have a green thumb. We'd feel a flood of mail will hit the U.S. Postal Service too. Whatever's defined as passion stopped at this town and has not moved on.

It was imperative, a blessing in disguise, and necessary as the iron cook stove, that they each take this year to strip down.

Chapter Twenty-two
Early Stills

Karyn must have died in a room beside a flickering blue flame. Blue was her color. Attended by none. So she must have realized her dream: to die at home. Rachel lay awake all night remembering Karyn's blue eyes: inky, the color of the blue glass dish she must have had beside her. She was somewhere, I think, past pain.

*

Still Three: "The Darkroom Continues"
Why do I call still one "Our Meeting" when it was of the darkroom, silvers shining up from the liquid? It has a wildness. I would have loved being a war photographer, been magnetized by the sky over London, ominous with blimps shining silver in sun. Like Walker Evans, I would have wowed them doing work for the Farm Security Administration. But in 1935 I was too young. Early photos were mainly of people, not portraits, not Eugène Atget–type sepias in which edges are softened. There Chel stands in her letter-carrier outfit. Foursquare, holding up the first-day issue of a stamp, her one braid pinned up. Another album leaf I turn. There I am on the day the dog died, our second sheepdog. "You take too many of me, Maggie," Chel complained. "Never," I smiled.

*

Still Four: "Nellie"
Here is our neighbor in Scarstown, Nellie, sixty-five at the time of my portrait. One dead chicken she holds in each hand. She holds a charmed expression, as if she would never expect to have her portrait taken. She was a platonic love, a flame of mine. Chel took loving swings at Nellie. Nellie's in civilization but holds a wilderness within. She is a loner. Her husband died twenty years ago. She is a loner with Bramble, her cat, and her chickens. The neighborhood kids call her Aunt Nellie and consume her cakes, custards, and puddings. I caught her in this moment of fierce energy and slightly barbaric exaltation after she had just wrung the neck of each bird. With bare gums, she resembles a Russian peasant woman, a woman warrior. The veins in her hand stand out. There is a history of many women in those hands. Blood is still under the nails.

145

Chapter Twenty-three
The Stone Eyeball

Still Five: "Corpses in Ginghams"
I feel hated, unloved. I'm running away," Erik said when he came
one day to our door after I'd sold some real estate. Maggie photographed
him. Hanging his head, he shuffled. I think she felt this way herself as
a girl. The boy child's face in the picture is a classic mask. Land. My eye
roves back over land. The way Margaret memorized its curves in black
and white, I learned the street by carrying mail.

"I fell," he said and curled up in a ball on our back stoop, Erik did,
and dug his head into his lap. Clenched fists. Maggith looked exhausted
after she took that shot. I guess she was in her mid-forties then but she
could shoot right back into being a child.

"Why not go in, Maggith, and lie down?"

"Ha! I'm hale as a horse."

"And pale as a ghost," I said, or something to that extent.

I stared hard at the lilacs on the wallpaper in the close, hot summer
kitchen of our old Widdershins. Who chose that old lilac wallpaper? The
house was built around 1922. Lilac must have been in. I recall the airless
feel to our kitchen that morning when Erik was hangdog. It's strange
what I remembered while shoveling snow and feeling good on this
morning. I am an old girl now. Whenever your mother dies, she leaves
you suddenly an orphan even if you're an old orphan. I worked to keep
the tenor of Maggie's life and mine gentle and sane even while I knew
the power and temperament of Maggie's gift. I stared down the angels,
those fierce stone angels she got from Stonehewer's Lane. I saw they were
often angels gone wrong. There was a sarcastic curl to the upper lip, a
glance of contempt in the stone eyeball.

Mother Karyn died beside a flickering blue flame. I consider Colette's
blue lantern. I see a blue flame flickering on lilac wallpaper and can
nearly smell musk in this cold room. Sitting on the edge of the cold
tub at night, I think about death. Consider death: what is that to this
thinking reed, a human? What was Jo's confessor like? I am jealous;
I wanted to be her confessor. She told me no more than the bird on
the branch tells the ice of its trembling. She slept in a brass bed. I can
smell the particular smell of the brass bedstead. I visualize the prayer of
St. Francis above her head, I can imagine the wood crucifix. Why am I
haunted by the mystery of religion? My father. I start reliving the slow
development of physical closeness between Maggie and me from the first
shy kiss stolen at the Y. I go out, bang in, pace from one room to the

other. Big wool flakes fall again out of a gray sky, a tumbling of feathers from a pillow. On such gray days Maggie would spring out the ancient ironing board scarred with iron and cigarette burns from the wall where it lived while more snow batted against the windowpanes. "Ironing?" I would ask. "Nope. We're having an indoor picnic." She'd set out a can of beer, a chunk of cheese and a slab of ham on the board. She wore her clown blouse, with purple and cream stripes and ruffled at the neck, which made her look like a ruffled grouse. Put an extra shot of iron in your backbone, woman.

JANET CLAY: SHOPKEEPER, LACES & LINEN became JANET CLAY: ANTIQUE DEALER. Her calling card changed. This floor heater turns a menacing red, working away beside Maggith's old black bike pump. I can't let go of all of her. This morning I checked up on Maude Nelson's house right by Olson's Dry Goods. Maude has been gone one month. I said I'd check to see if a thief had broken in or not. As I looked into the sky, I saw next door, ten ginghams blowing: dresses, blouses, shirts, blue-checked and red. Frozen-stiff gingham corpses.

In Little Norway, Turret Street has all the antique shops. I'm going to take these sore feet and walk them down Turret Street. The vision of frozen gingham encourages me to think Maggie has gained some from entering her wilderness for all I have paid. I, too, may have gained, although I wouldn't have chosen a wreckage of emotion. Every time I imagine contentment it takes the shape of shared life between two women. The star quilt is its icon. Winter is the gathering time.

The waits were long between mails. I carried sacks all my working life and grew stir-crazy, so I took up Japanese then dropped it because learning languages was not my forte.

Dear Maggie,
I am caught in some strange bafflement. We need more tenderness as we grow older, not a division of ways. I enjoy crossword puzzles but relish even more a thousand-piece jigsaw puzzle. I find the white sail tip, which completes the regatta. I turn tail from loneliness but do not run. I'd rather get this auto started than sit in the drive all day...

She broke off the letter. Why do folk call life a journey when it is a struggle? Where are we getting? She took up the pen again.

... Bree just rang, so I had a bit of a distraction. Like you, Mag, I always have a village inside my head. My life is a very quiet one, but my brain is a convivial meeting place. I did Pawnshop Row today where the movie palace is, and stepped into Experienced Clothes. The people who

run the twice-around clothes are new friends in my life. Chelsea, who
sells clothing by day, is a bartender at night. Lindsy, Chelsea's partner,
devotes all her time to Experienced Clothes, which used to be called
Second Hand Rose. They have a madcap love, but their languages don't
mix and marry as ours did. You found your solemn and sad vision
of America composed of dreams realized and dreams gone bad. The
time between wars was no slumber but it was brief. I sleep too often.
I throw open the window at night and see the bottom of the Little
Dipper dive into the elms. Big trees. Small minds. That's our town.
You photographed children and came up with those who foreshadowed
betrayal in their gaze.

Always thinking of you, Maggie.

Yours, Rachel

*

Still Six: "Black Book"

Chel's mother bequeathed Rachel a journal, a black book, and little
else aside from her courage. Oh, yes, she bequeathed her a porcelain
Christmas tree, which Chel looked at now on the kitchen table while
she typed over her handwritten letter. As letters back and forth became
more regular, she switched to the old Underwood. It shook when Rachel
pounced on it with sturdy strikes. Had she been in a long, colonial
silence, letter-writing only in sleep all these years? On this typewriter
Chel hammered out her column on plants. She watched cautiously as
their newly established correspondence grew and her column lengthen.
As a mail carrier she used to notice, when letters grew more often
between people. Sometimes letters crossed the Boundary Waters, that
mystical thing between the States and Canada. More fun was watching a
correspondence grow to the point where you were certain a romance was
brewing.

When I handled letters, it was a laying on of hands. The job was
complex enough that I had to keep all my wits about me. Karyn was
always a genius with a penny, a dime. She had us taste things in small
portions. She had served food to Dolly and me on dishes just a tad larger
than the tea plates that our dolls ate off of in our doll house.

But it was known in Little Norway that one should beware of getting
on my wrong side. I flamed like an angered lion, sent gold sparks into the
atmosphere like a medieval fireside in December. Threatened folk, like
scared animals, show their worst side. But this was primarily the marrow
in the broth, which made the flavor that laced the stew.

Rachel noted repetitions and reflections. The typewriter, which freed her letters to Maggie, had a kin in the camera, which in turn had a kin with the boxed clock that told the actual time. The sack in which letters were hauled with its weary generosities was her badge.

The spiritual time came last; that was the time she was clocking now.

"I didn't have a classic childhood in spite of being always lonely," Maggie said.

"I was a child who dreamed of running away to sea," Chel said. "Did you ever?" asked Maggie. "You know the answer," Chel smiled. That was how she fit the fifth box into her life as she readied to enter the seventh jump.

They'd been radio kids. It filled Rachel and Maggie's evening with drama and lyricism. They lay and listened to the wireless. Churchill's voice was buried in the tubes, in their history. Chel would go into the kitchen, make a big bang, and pour oil in the kettle to pop corn. "A lark!" she'd laugh her rumbly low laugh, which always thrilled Maggie. "It's a lark, darling," They'd eat the popcorn heavily salted, smelling of oil, with the low thunder of voices rumbled over the radio. The room was dark and all the popcorn was gone. They'd gone to heaven and died. Sometimes they sleep in the living room, hauling the old star quilt from their bed. Maggie woke and doused the last of the fire with the last of the tea. These were their most intense moments, when time, like a still lake, lay suspended, able to reflect houses, brick churches down to every last pearl of stone. The lake was an encyclopedia then.

*

"Work, worship, play," hummed Chel one afternoon. A radiance came from each woman. It was an ordinary evening, but only a quarter of them was in the present. The rest was in the past, which totally wrapped up their attention. "You are an inspired person," Chel had said. Maggie knew it was like sunset and would be gone.

"Paul Revere!" Chel teased Maggith, who had put on her tricorn hat tonight.

"I feel like a rebel," Maggith had said and closed the door to her darkroom with a click.

The darkroom was a private chapel with its own secular ceremonies. Such nights used all four quarters of the mind. When Mag appeared at breakfast the next morning, she shrugged, shook her head, and said, "No longer exhilarated," signaling an end to this episode of her otherworldly time.

Conclusion
The Final Stills

The bed will fill up with letters: red-and-blue airmail in Maggie's cabin. In Widdershins, too, it was becoming a labor sorting them. Each woman was sorting the early letters from the late letters that came with the recent influx. Rachel was cataloging the letters. Despite the odd pang in her side, she had again taken up smoking Gauloises, those French cigarettes with woody tobacco that crumbled in the fingers. They came in a cellophane-wrapped light-blue packet with blue helmet on the front. The front room of Widdershins filled with the heady tobacco scent. These had been Maggie's favorite cigarettes. She was feeling something akin to inspiration.

Janet Clay had a few plates, very few, which when turned over read ENOCH WOODS, ENGLISH SCENERY, WOODS & SONS, ENGLAND. Chel had only these very few letters from Maggith, written from the cabin. She handled with the care one used to turned Enoch Woods plate over to read the artisan's mark.

Her back itself felt stronger. Her neck would never be right again. She ran her hand along the nape of her neck. She drank more brandy these nights than she had with Maggie. She got into smoking, writing, dashing out a note to Maggie with gusto, and answered the phone with irritation. Her paranoia, her obsession with being outcast, ostracized by the village increased, turning days to pewter. That antisocial beast was stirring in her again. She remembered the same hot itch when she had to track an express mail international parcel for an author on the other end of the phone. January closed up the earth like sealing wax closes an envelope. Nothing, not even Burleson's snoring or batting a monster in his dream could break her concentration. She thought maybe she was falling in love again. I will tell no one, she vowed, least of all Margaret herself. It is strange. Salt and grace filled her face. Trafalgar Square came back, when she laid her head back on the old ladder-back chair; she took off her glasses and in a sharp, visionary dream experienced pain.

Maggie didn't have what one might call an Irish nose, one that was slightly upturned. But she had the grace of the sea in those green eyes. It was more a Roman nose. When Chel went about muffling tenderness in gruffness, it galled Maggie. I have gained the confidence to speak my heart, Chel decided now in age. These were the cold, flat months in which one could work on oneself in order to strengthen and shine. During the few hours when the small world of her town and her yard

at Widdershins were sunlit, it looked as though a printer's box of
lead numerals and letters had been pulled out and were on display to
onlookers in the bronze light of an otherworldly sun.

Maggie rode the tide waiting for fresh letters. Each woman knew how
to channel her energy into other avenues than her chosen ones, but the
very rare hours when Maggie and Rachel could pick up the other's radar
were the best hours. It is as though I stand under the low-flying Halley's
Comet, Maggie thought, and I saw each grain of dirt or steel shavings the
lathe had made bathed in light. Long ago they had sat up in bed nursing
brandy and cigarettes before Chel had once more kicked the habit.
Maggie never even tried. Margaret's long fingers turned the Gauloises
carefully, quizzically. "If you had cancer and thought that kicking the
habit would get you off the hook, would you quit?"

"Hard to say," Maggie answered. To crawl out of the tight box into
the bright air of freedom. Was it worth giving up the razor edge of free
choice? Chel continued smoking, enjoying every minute. Teal winter
night shut her in a box.

"I break two resolutions constantly," Rachel said, rising and stubbing
out her cigarette. "I resolve not to smoke in bed"

"And the other?" Maggie asked. "Not to think in bed."

"You know Bree considered suicide when she felt caught between two
rocks: love and another country."

"I would never," answered Chel." If you love enough, you will stay for
the one you love."

Maggie had bought a black block of Japanese ink in order to do
Sumi painting with a brush. Maggie recalled the liquor cabinet back in
Widdershins; it was the apple crate in their hall closet beside the giant
jam jar filled with assorted old rubber bands. She dreamed of coming
home to a celebration at the restaurant where she'd taken Chel for her
fiftieth. One of the great old American railroads that ran through Little
Norway. The Chalet was at the end of the line, where she dreamed of
a meal fit for kings. The high beams had a rosiny smell, and there was
always a roaring fire in winter. In spring and summer there was a pond
that housed goldfish who floated dreamily to the surface. It offered
British delicacies like liver pâté with pistachio nuts ground up in it, cold
beef Wellington, cold ham, and hot steak-and-kidney pies, assorted salads
with homemade mayonnaise. To start, you had your choice of French
onion soup or New England clam chowder. To close, there was always
freshly baked pie or tarts, whichever you preferred, in addition to a
lemon chiffon so creamy your fork floated through it.

Townson came up to Maggie, purring as though she could smell the
feast through Maggie's reverie. All was served silently, which is the best

kind of service, Karyn always said. Chel was an old puritan who believed in self-control to the nth degree: put the savage down despite indulging one's gustatory sense to the highest point, where it was an art. This restaurant was where Chel had exclaimed, "Venison, my love," and later speculated upon how the animal was shot. Was he running over grasses?

The meal was a legend between the two. It was where Chel had observed that one always wants a bit of wild water when one has grown up with wild water. The ritual, elegance, and harmony of the restaurant went with the subdued chamber music. They were both old radio children now. Could they return to such a swanky place, or would they be more comfortable in a small pub off Oslo Square? When they had left the restaurant after Chel's fiftieth, it was under the spell of the Cheshire cat. Chel had worn her burgundy velvet, a sort of hunting jacket affair. She looked like a riding mistress in spite of the fact that she sat wrong when she rode and horses dropped her off at posts and rubbed her off on iron gates. Maggie had looked somewhat like a country squire wearing impossible green, a shade neither loud nor soft. That occasion was now twenty years in the past. Now was the time for basic black and pearls. Maggie scarfed up her food wearing only a paisley scarf, and nobody made a crack when she pulled out her checkbook.

Down in town Rachel thought that death cannot make all this unrecognizable. It will always blaze vividly: our kitchen, the excited heart beating. Death and age cannot quell the brash wit or quiet anticipation. Death is among us but vanquished in the company of such women as we are.

Yet Karyn was gone, Helga was gone. When Karyn lay in the hospital, Chel pressed her close. Her mother's words had been, "This one I want to take with me." Of Karyn's children, including Dolly who had died, Chel was the strongest, with a severe strength. During the stern, harsh summer, we were saved by cat-sitting. Chelsea and Lindsy would take off for the Shakespeare festival up north and leave us to look after Mirthless and Quincy. Mirthless was the cat who never purred, and Quincy loved quince jam. Tonight each woman, musing, came to the same fork in the road. The Stratford Festival in Canada. To sit in a setting divorced from one's history or one's partner puts one in an otherworldly space. Photos, paintings, shawls flashed through each woman's mind.

Karyn never took Rachel to Stratford in Ontario or England. She never visited the Lake District, Folkestone, Huddersfield, Yorkshire. Yet she wanted to take me into heaven when Lady Death came. Our bones betray us. The body holds its own clock. We say goodbye. Chel still had not heard the results of her mid-December ultrasound. There were no

assurances. She closed her eyes, smiling at the portraits Maggie took of
Mother Karyn. "Marvels. So many! She's worth more."

Maggie had taken a charcoal stick and drawn a circle. There was a
center of love, of courage but no set radius. She looked at Townson
and knew she must begin to pack. She swept up the letters that covered
her bed. She had grown up; the child with pipe-stem legs was running,
walking. An hour after her final still was shot she was on her feet shadow
boxing like the boy Erik who felt detested, abandoned.

*

Still Seven: "Civilization, the Schoolroom"

Maggie was in a schoolroom, a mob of small toughs lined up for a
spelling bee, all with their fists behind their backs, ready to spin a yarn.
She saw them now as a houseful of ghosts, little apple women who
pursued her some nights in her dreams. Chel's mother used to tell her
daughter that she had a will of iron: "It glows when it's heated." Maggie
thought of the star quilt, as she drew back the covers, crawled under
them, and slept. When she swam, Maggie wore a leotard and did long
laps. Chel wore those gruesome shapeless tank suits that graced, or
disgraced, beaches in the twenties. Maggie was a long-distance swimmer;
Chel did the dog paddle. Chel thought of sand as she sorted letters,
old from new, and rubber-banded them. The star quilt was draped over
the bed. Despite the fact that the stars were cloth, they shone. Maggie
had a quilt with blues and reds. She detested patriotic quilts, but as she
squinted, the tints softened. The gray lamb hot bot was back home.
Chel had probably filled him with water from the kettle, the covered
hot-water bottle that lived on a peg in the bathroom in their old home,
Widdershins.

She had a vision of Dolly, her twin, who long ago drowned in
childhood on a summer afternoon. Flooded in childhood, the girl
surfaced tonight. Revenant, Dolly would remain forever platinum.
Sheltering yet shuddering under the quilt, Rachel recalled the dream
with the vividness, as if a match had lit the scene of those trunks with
pullout drawers her father and mother had that the twins adored. They
would build constructs out of childhood's imagination: caves like the
knee holes of desks, the wings of the trunk that when opened would
have an army blanket draped across the top. Her six-foot frame, a bulk
like a mountain or a cloud, shifted around as if of its own accord. Other
than that, there was little movement.

Her lady's taken another mate, went through Maggie's dream. So did
Sister Jo, whom she had not seen in a year. Her hair was feathered like
a sparrow's feathers, with bolts of white running through it. We cause

ourselves misery when we box ourselves in. I tend to give up the power
in a relationship. Did Maggie? She had mustered more power in her exile
and so had more in hand.

> *Ich am of Irelaund*
> *and of the Holy Launde*
> *Come out of charity*
> *And daunce with me in Irelaund.*

That's what those gray eyes of Jo's said. Cats sat frozen on sills in
winter, feeling the warmth of the fire at their backs. Maggie awoke
looking at Townson. Townson and Burleson would be together again
soon. She finished packing and wrote the letter to the college. Cats
contained the mystery of us all.

She reminisced on that afternoon that she and Dolly had ventured
up in the attic and discovered Mrs. Pearl Patch. The dining room ceiling
had reminded them of the planetarium. In the gray-washed prairie light,
they had leafed through copies of the *Sears, Roebuck Catalogue*. Seedlings
of light sprouted along with the ice spines in the kitchen window. There
was a cold wind. It was November. They had looked up to wheels of
spider webs. The light was the color of dark tea to child eyes. There exists
no photograph. But picture to yourself two spindly legged children in the
Nebraska light in the early years of the twentieth century.

Teach me, Chel thought, as she made peace and rose. Teach me the
peace that passes understanding. There was a call—from the lab. "The
doctor wants you to come in as soon as possible." It passes understanding
this peace, but where does it go? Understanding was the one thing
Solomon asked of the king of heaven. The body could and would be
slowed down, but the soul could never be incarcerated. She was a living
testament to that with her body failing, her humors, her economies, her
dream of walking into the snow until she no longer felt.

Chel put up the morning kettle, the battered old one she and
Maggith called Elliot. FALL IN LOVE AGAIN read the maple leaf pin from
Canada that Bree wore home. Finally the struggle had released bars and
let light in, though in unexpected fashion. What message might she get
from the laboratory? What if Maggie were to come home? Would it be
as comfortable as it was in the beginning? She was not getting what she
fought for. By relenting, giving up all fight, after losing and returning,
in her loss there might be some gain. She had gained the confidence to
speak her mind. Maggie would look so dashing smoking like Lili Marleen
leaning against the lamp post, raising her face to her soldier boy in war,
light pouring down on her like a benediction.

I feel like a burned-out ember. What would Dolly have resembled in a windbreaker, strolling along with me at age sixteen, nineteen, and twenty-one? Would we have been mirror images, both tall with ash-brown hair and hazel eyes.

When Maggie relented from efforts of her art, what then? Profound letdown. Time and again she would explain to me that black and white has a spiritual quality.

"I'm battling my way into a fresh vision." She told me about silver tints slowly, patiently, how they began. The silvers in the needlepoint ivy, which was flourishing, magnetized her. The silvers crouched in the plant could leap forth from the chemicals in the pan. Did Chel see? When she was close to death, my mother pictures a woman in a brown derby riding depicted on batik of blown silk toward the sun. Karyn's woman went bolting like a shot clear through death. She was stronger, that rider, than geographies in the butterscotch schoolroom of my early times. The century and I were young then.

What if her soldier girl was coming home after a long journey of self-awakening? She might need all the well wishes she could get come next week. "Hold still!" "I can't hold still."

There was a river that ran through the town called Little Norway. Its name was Peace. Chel lost sight of it in her sixty-ninth year and gained the sight of it again in her seventieth.

In the seventh jump, when the cord rope whacked on the dirt of the grammar school playground, the faces of the children tightened, blanched as if bleached with white flour or dusted with death itself. The superstition was that if you missed this one bad luck would be yours. In the seventh jump of life the faces Chel saw about her were preparing for eternity. She has reached the confidence to speak her heart.

The six points of the star, which was the icon for her life, were bleached but as recognizable as Dolly's face, revenant, her twin, who had threaded her life like the greenhouse, the darkroom. Next it is Petré, spiritual twin to Dolly, who felt out our faces with his hands and read them. Now it is Petré, our boy, whom we could never adopt outside his hospital stretcher and bed.

Now it is he, he alone, who exemplifies that saying "Happiness is for humans, not for angels." Did he ever know happiness? Or only ecstasy, bliss? He never had a little dog to shadow him; nurses shadowed him,

doctors with stethoscopes and charts. Fever thermometers told the story
of his days, not a journal kept in schoolboy cursive. He never saw his
face in the mirror. He read voices as other children read books or nuns
read devotional texts. He read voices the way Rachel reads addresses on
envelopes. But when Maggie or Rachel touched his foot on the stretcher,
he would said, "Maggie, how are you?" or "Rachel, how are you?"

Several times Chel or Maggie told the ward nurse that Petré wanted
to make a phone call. "How can he?" the nurse asked incredulously. "He
can." He weighed only eighty-five pounds, although he was fourteen
years old. As he lay trembling on his back on the plinth, either Rachel
or Maggie would push him to the telephone at the nurse's station.
Whichever woman was paying the visit to the children's hospital would
dial home, with the other partner waiting there to receive the call. Like
Dolly, he died still in childhood, but Petré died from a seizure at the end
of his fourteenth year. He had been singing "Amazing Grace" in his high
piping boy soprano, perfectly in tune. Earlier that day, he had belted out
with particular ardor words from the song, "I was blind who now can
see."

Like Juliet, he rounded his fourteenth year with passion. For Chel,
he remains among the living, always among the living. No revenant.
Speaking in fits and starts, he is blind, but his hands are forming a star
as his fingers flex. Then his trembling hands fall back at his sides to
his white gown, pinning him like a boy angel of eleven, not so much
disabled as trapped. He is blind, but he sees. He raises his piping voice in
"Amazing Grace." Carved out of the hollow of grief, he felt his parents
fall through the crack in the world through which the light shines, as
the light shines on the bones of the greenhouse. Light. Sight. That was
all Chel wanted. "I did not control the savage beast in me enough," she
decided. I was blind who now can see with my own aged grace. My eyes
are poor, my eyes are old, but I pray my vision lasts the longest.

About the Author

Lynn Strongin was born in New York City in 1939 and was raised in and around New York. She lived in California during the politically active sixties and worked in Berkeley for Denise Levertov. During that turbulent period, she also met Robert Duncan, Josephine Miles, and Kay Boyle. She moved to Albuquerque, New Mexico, in the Seventies, and to British Columbia in 1979 where, for the past three decades she has made her home, although she considers herself profoundly to be an American writer.

Lynn has published twelve books, including the anthology *The Sorrow Psalms* (University of Iowa Press), *The Dwarf Cycle* (Thorp Springs Press), *Toccata of the Disturbed Child* (Fallen Angel Press), *A Hacksaw Brightness* (Ironwood Press), and *Countrywoman / Surgeon* (L'Epervier Press), all published in the Seventies, and *Bones and Kim: A Novella* (Spinster's Ink Press, 1980), and two new books, *Cape Seventy (Poems)* and *Crazed By the Sun: Poems of Ecstasy.* Lynn serves as Special Guest Editor for *New Works Review.* She has been nominated five times for a Pushcart Prize.

www.ingramcontent.com/pod-product-compliance
Lightning Source LLC
Chambersburg PA
CBHW072145130726
47909CB00004BB/1165